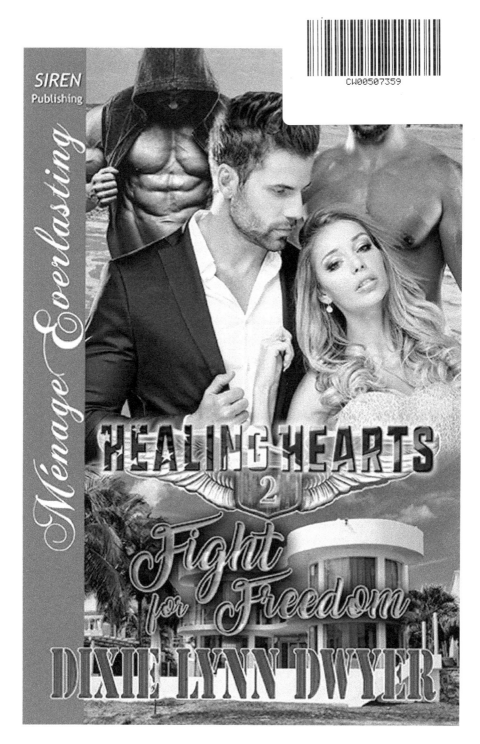

SIREN
Publishing

Ménage Everlasting

HEALING HEARTS
2
Fight for Freedom

DIXIE LYNN DWYER

Healing Hearts 2: Fight for Freedom

North has a secret. She is in hiding in Mercy, South Carolina after surviving being abused, drugged, and sold to a drug dealing terrorist by her own brother. Her scars run deep but she is determined to live a somewhat normal life, even knowing that she might forever be looking over her shoulder waiting for Forester to find her and take her back. She's established a real estate career, has made good friends, and keeps to herself.

Until her friend's three cousins return from a mission and seem to show interest in her. One thing leads to another, and not only is she fighting for her freedom, and trying to keep them unaware of her past to keep them alive, but she is being hunted, and as she lets down her guard, Forester attacks.

It's a race against time to locate her in Costa Rica, but her men are resourceful, and there's nothing a bunch of crazy determined mercenaries won't do to get their woman back in their arms and kill the man who holds her life in his hands.

Genre: Contemporary, Ménage a Quatre, Romantic Suspense
Length: 35,059 words

HEALING HEARTS 2: FIGHT FOR FREEDOM

Dixie Lynn Dwyer

Siren Publishing, Inc.
www.SirenPublishing.com

A SIREN PUBLISHING BOOK

HEALING HEARTS 2: FIGHT FOR FREEDOM
Copyright © 2018 by Dixie Lynn Dwyer

ISBN: 978-1-64243-380-7

First Publication: July 2018

Cover design by Les Byerley
All art and logo copyright © 2018 by Siren Publishing, Inc.

PUBLISHER
Siren Publishing, Inc.
www.SirenPublishing.com

DEDICATION

Dear readers,

Thank you for purchasing this legal copy of *Fight for Freedom*.

Healing a broken heart and soul is not an easy process. It takes time to heal, and being around the right people can help immensely. It can help a woman to forget a man who broke her heart, destroyed her self confidence, and scarred her soul, so that she can move on and be free to love again if she so chooses.

North is on a journey to forget, to heal, and appreciate being alive. So when she begins to have feelings for three men she hardly knows, she panics, because not only does she feel she has no right to care, anyone close to her will become the hunted, too, and will die for loving her.

May you enjoy her journey, as the power of love, and the determination of three resourceful men, pick up the pieces of her broken heart, teach her to trust and love again, and move heaven and earth to save her from the one man who's responsible for all her pain.

Happy reading.
HUGS!
Dixie

TABLE OF CONTENTS

HEALING HEARTS 2: FIGHT FOR FREEDOM

DIXIE LYNN DWYER

Chapter One

North Canty shuddered in the dark corner of the basement. There was nowhere else to turn to hide from his wrath.

"North, come to me now and I'll go easy on you," Forester yelled to her. She could hear his footsteps. Hear his strong accent. He was getting closer.

She slid down against the corner of the wall behind the boxes. Her face throbbed, her lips and her eyes swelled, and there was this pinching pain in them. He attacked her, beat her, and she barely escaped his rage. That pinky ring he wore scratched her neck. She clenched her eyes closed and wished he wouldn't find her.

The party was going on upstairs. People saw what he did, what he said to her and how he struck her. She didn't know if she were better off running or remaining there where witnesses were. What if he drugged her? These men drugged women all the time and took what they wanted. He'd done that to her before, to make her comply to his wishes, his games.

Since no one intervened, no one would dare defy Forester, she ran through the house. His buddies blocked the door at the kitchen, and she was so scared she ran down the stairs to the basement, past the people playing pool, and enjoying the game room and went way back into the unfinished part. They looked at her but then heard Forester yelling and they froze. They went back to playing. They would be no help to her. She hurried through the doorway to the part of the basement that had sliding glass doors she could escape through. She gasped when she saw through the glass, Gordo and Pulta, guards of Forester, standing there blocking it.

She jumped as the door to this side of the basement slammed closed. She couldn't breathe. Her heart was racing, and there was no one to help her. This was it. Forester was going to kill her.

She cuddled in the corner, her knees to her chest. She was caught in a world that would be the death of her. Perhaps today was the day.

"I hear your breathing. You caused a scene up there, and you disobeyed an order. You don't run away from me, North!" He yelled his words in anger, and she jerked when she heard the slap of his belt against his hand. She clenched her swollen eyes tight and started to rock and beg for someone to help her. How did she wind up here? How did she wind up being the obsession of Forester Colon?

She made so many mistakes. She fell for his lies, his charms, his money and his promise to help clear her brother Tyler's debt to some South American terrorist. Tears poured from her eyes. Forester killed Tyler. Her brother was dead, and she wanted nothing to do with Forester now, with these people he surrounded himself with, and tonight she planned on leaving. She didn't want to believe Forester's words, his revelation that Tyler sold her off to Forester. *My brother sold me to this monster? How could you do that to me? How could you make me part of this? I'm a human being. You can't sell a human being.*

She screamed as he grabbed her arm and yanked her up, making it feel like her arm pulled from the socket, and his fingers capable of crushing her bones. He backhanded her in the mouth and she swung to the left, hit the wall, and placed her palms against it.

"No, Forester, please. I can't take it. Please let me go. You can have any woman you want." She sobbed, her cheek against the concrete wall of the basement.

He was on her so fast, so abruptly. He shoved her hard against the wall, her chin slamming into the concrete.

"No!" she screamed, and then the strikes came. The belt slapped against her body, then came the threats, the scent of his expensive cologne, and the sound of his accent and deep voice into her ear.

"You are mine, North. How dare you think for one moment you could break things off with me. I hold your life in my hands. In my hands!" he screamed into her hair. His spittle hit her cheek and she cried, sobbing while he stroked her skin with the leather of the belt. His other hand slid along her waist and he pulled her back against his front.

She gasped in fear of this man and his capabilities, and the pain his movements caused. Her ribs had to be broken, she was seriously injured she just knew it, but he didn't care. He'd put her in a hospital and even there no one would help her. Money bought everything and everyone. She could barely see through her swollen eyes, but she felt his touch. His command over her body as he spoke. "I'm never going to let you go. You are my possession. My woman, you belong to Forester Colon now and forever."

He slid fingers between her legs and sucked her skin on her neck. She couldn't even catch her breath. Her heart raced, her body shook in trepidation. He was breathing through his nostrils as his phone rang but he ignored it. He squeezed her breast hard and then pulled back and unleashed more punishments on her until that ringing phone stopped him from continuing.

"You've made me so very angry, North. Very, very angry. You know there's so much going on right now. Tonight you suffer the consequences of crossing me and trying to leave." He pulled back, then the other two guards of his reached for her. She was in so much pain. She couldn't walk as they held her upright.

"Get her to the car and bring her to the warehouse. Castella will finish things up here and close down the house. You make sure the jet is ready for our flight. Clean her up, and tie her to the bed on the plane. By the time we're in South America, she'll be fully committed and know the rules."

They nodded, lifted her up, and headed out of the basement through the sliding glass doors.

His cell phone rang again.

* * * *

"Forester, we have a situation."

"With what?" he asked, heading through the game room, looking at his fist, and the damaged knuckles from striking North so hard. She enraged him. He didn't know how she found out that her brother was dead, but it didn't matter. She would be his forever. Tyler sold her to him to help pay for his fuck ups.

"Tyler wasn't working alone."

"What the fuck does that mean, Castella?"

"Another federal agent was aware of him and the fact that Tyler was working undercover, and worked for us. The buzz is the feds are coming for you."

He stopped short, and his temper flared. His first thoughts left his lips. "Did North know?"

"I haven't gotten that far, but might I suggest you get on that fucking plane and do it fast. There was a situation in Peru. Some government operatives infiltrated the facility. Ferlong and the others aren't responding."

He started to move faster through the house then to the waiting vehicle. "Son of bitch. Federal agents?"

"'Military. Mercenaries or something. It's a fucking mess and the product, all gone. They confiscated everything. It's a mess. Federal agents are dead, some military, too, and all the men working for us dead or they disappeared. Like I said, no word on Ferlong."

"Fuck. I want to know who and I want them dead. I need to know if North was part of this. I'm sure Ferlong escaped. He never remains too close by when operations are running. He would have had some sort of indication that there was going to be a raid. We've got people keeping ears and eyes open. I need to know if North was aware of this."

"I don't think she was. She's twenty-two and her brother backstabbed the agency he worked for and then wound up in debt to Loconto, besides you and Ferlong. Seems he was working all angles to buy his freedom. That's what I have thus far."

"Loconto? Holy fuck. Dumb fucking agent. Does Loconto know about North?"

"I don't know. Just get the hell out of there please. If the feds grab you—"

"They won't. I'll be on the plane within the hour, and with North."

He ended the call and then dialed the men who just took North. No one answered. He tried again, and again, as he headed with his security guys to the SUV to leave for the airport.

"Forester!"

He turned to look at Synista, his main guard who was on the phone.

"The cottage is surrounded. Federal agents. The guys are dead."

"North?"

"Nothing. We don't know."

"Fuck!" he screamed out and slammed his hands down on the leather seats, gripping the edge and rocking and roaring in anger. "She is mine. I need her. I am not giving her up. She is mine."

His men looked on and nodded, and Forester's heart hammered inside of his chest. He finally broke her down, beat her, and would continue that training so she knew she was his and only his. He had to have her. He should have kept her by his side. He had seen the way she acted the last few days. She was pulling away from him and he wondered if Tyler told her what he had done? Could he have? She seemed so shocked when Forester revealed the truth to her. That her brother sold her to him to cover his debt and to make amends for what Forester tried to do to help him. Bad thing was, Tyler was caught stealing from Forester. The asshole thought he could double play all of them. Maybe turn Castella and Loconto against him. Asshole didn't know about loyalty and business. This was business and no woman, no emotions, would keep any of them from conducting their business and gaining money and power to dominate. Tyler was dead wrong.

Forester felt the SUV moving quickly. His tracks were covered though. The feds had nothing on him. Tyler, even if he ratted Forester out, was dead now, so what would it matter? The feds couldn't prove a thing. His hands were clean, but they could have North. What would North tell them? How much did she know? He never had her in the room for any discussions. She was his possession and became his possession so quickly he had her on a pedestal. He wanted to hold onto her innocence, like he held onto her virginity, took it, claimed her body, and would be the only man to have her. Fuck. What if this took time to get her back? What if he never saw her again and she fucked some other man? The rage built up instantly.

"Fuck!" he roared, and he could see his men's expressions of concern. They knew his wrath. Someone was going to die. Many were going to die because of this.

He thought of North. He needed her, wanted her, and he would have her again.

My lover, I will get you back. No matter how long it takes, I'll get you back.

* * * *

"*What do you have for me, Selasi?*" Mike asked over the satellite phone.

"*This guy Ferlon has done deals with Castella.*"

"Are you serious? Do you think Castella is there, where we're headed?"

"Could be, so might I suggest you watch your asses. I know your mission is about this guy working with Ferlong and taking them both into custody, but if they have some help from Castella and his backing, who the fuck knows what you six are walking into."

"Got it. Thanks for the heads up. We'll call when we're done."

"Be safe."

"Roger that."

"What did Selasi say about Castella?" Phantom asked him. Mike looked at him, then Turner, Watson, and Dell.

"Ferlong does business with Castella. That could be the additional men and SUV parked outside of that warehouse," Watson whispered.

"Could be, and what a fucking catch," Fogerty added.

"Our mission is to take in Ferlong. If Castella is there then it's an added bonus."

"Then let's do this. Be smart, and don't get dead," Dell said to them. They chuckled and agreed, and then prepared to enter the warehouse.

As they approached on all angles, their infiltration turned into a nightmare. They weren't the only ones there. Before they could even move into position they saw the black jackets, the yellow lettering.

"FBI? Fuck," he said aloud.

"What do we do?" Dell asked.

Shots started to hit the dirt around them. Spotlights illuminated their location and it was do or die as they returned fire and took out anyone in their path.

"Get down!" Dell yelled out, but the shots hit them, sending them onto their asses. The bulletproof vest protected most of their bodies. Mike roared and so did Phantom and Turner, and they got back up and saw the federal agents going down. One by one they were killed by these terrorist drug dealing assholes. It was a fucking massacre. "Kill *them fucking all!" he roared, and they fired their weapons taking out the guards, the ones that shot at them and killed the agents.*

It was a blur of smoke, death, and the scent of fumes from the drugs made his head feel fuzzy. He heard the yelling. He saw the agents dead, shots to their heads, their bodies. Then more were shot by some guy yelling.

"You're dead! He will hunt you down and kill you all. You're dead!" the guy yelled at them, and then began to fire his weapon.

They returned fire, killing him as others came running toward them. They all took hits and Mike prayed that everyone was okay as they were the last men standing. He looked around them. Absorbed the silence, the scene of violence, war, the mission a nightmare, and then to his team. Everyone was injured. Blood, exhaustion, and then Turner tumbled by the stairs, holding his side, a knife protruding from it. The nightmare had only just begun. Chaos erupted everywhere. More men were coming to kill them.

"Turner!"

Mike awoke, taking a moment to regain his mind and realize that it was that repeat nightmare from over two years ago. He fell asleep in the recliner watching t.v. and his mind went back to that fucking shit show. Bad intel, too many players, and a situation that haunted their minds. They almost lost Turner, who took a bullet to his shoulder and a knife to his side, and Phantom who was held at gunpoint and beaten until Mike and the rest of the team located him and rescued him. It was not supposed to go down that way. He sat up and rubbed his chin.

Ferlong was nowhere to be found. They thought he was dead. Not a chance. The son of a bitch escaped. Him, as well as Phantom, wanted to be the one to kill him, but it didn't look like they would get their chance. That operation could have cost all their lives. Now he chose carefully. Which jobs, which location, and what they entailed with him and the team's safety top priority.

They weren't getting any younger and being around Mercy and all this town had to offer was starting to make them think about retirement.

They could do things like Selasi did, and work intel in the safe, relaxing atmosphere of their own homes. Going out in a blaze of glory no longer had the same appeal. Especially leading up to that shit show in Peru. The abused women, the forced laborers, all in the name of some drug dealer and terrorist who was using the money to buy weapons and build his army of rebels. It was all so confusing and complicated. It wasn't like they were just terrorists from one cell. No, these men, this group, came from different areas in the Middle East as well as South America. What were the fucking South Americans doing joining forces with terrorist? There had to be some sort of dealings going on but what? Something more than drugs and guns? What could it be? He racked his brain like he did every time that mission came back to his mind. It was over. Just leave it behind them and move on. He had to, as a leader and man who wanted more for his team.

His cell phone rang and he stretched out his muscles and answered it. "Yo," he said into it.

"Guess who I'm looking at right fucking now?" Turner said to him.

"Got no idea."

"Rodriguez."

Mike sat up. "No."

"Yes I am. Him and Denver are in town visiting Denver's sister and her husband. They want to meet up tonight. You game?" Turner asked.

"Hell yeah. I'll talk to Phantom."

"I told them that Watson, Dell, and Fogerty are out of town. I'll come back to the house in a little bit once I confirm plans."

"Sounds good, Turner."

Mike ended the call and smiled, shaking his head. He hadn't seen Rodriguez and Denver in a long time. He thought they retired from the military and was working in the police department in New Jersey or something after a stint with the FBI. He would love to catch up with them. This call definitely changed his mood for the better.

* * * *

"Yes, ma'am, the kitchen is extra-large and great for entertaining. Of course, that view out the back and the beach in the distance is an added bonus," North said to the woman as her and her husband walked around the upscale beach home.

North heard her cell phone go off again and assumed it was either April or Afina texting about tonight. Smiling, she glanced down and felt her coloring go and that fearful sensation hit her in the chest. She glanced up at the clients who were now on the patio looking impressed.

The phone went off again.

Just checking in. No need to panic. Would love to hear your voice and confirm all is good.

She exhaled, feeling a slight bit of relief hearing from Sebastian Mount. He was a federal agent who worked with her brother Tyler. He was the reason why she was alive today and placed into hiding here in Mercy. His Uncle Billy and Aunt Stella lived twenty minutes from town. All of North's friends she made out here so far believe that Billy and Stella were North's aunt and uncle. Well, she considered them family. They were the closest she had to relatives. That thought made her think of Tyler.

She took a moment to text Sebastian, letting him know she was with clients but would text as soon as she was finished.

The couple walked back into the house, grabbing her full attention.

"We want to make an offer. What do you think is fair, North? We don't want to mess around and waste time."

She smiled. "I know the seller wanted as close to asking price as possible, but they did price it to sell. I wouldn't go too low."

She spent the next thirty minutes going over their offer, signing some papers, and then told them she would be in touch as soon as she got a response.

They left the house and she remained there making the call to the other realtor and the offer. He would contact the sellers and hopefully North made another great sale. She really loved the community, and hoped to one day have a home of her own here, but condo life was the best for her right now. She didn't sleep well, liked the idea of being on the eighth floor overlooking the ocean and having only one way in and out of her condo. The front door.

I'm good now.

She texted Sebastian, and a minute later her phone rang. She couldn't help but get that nervous, anxious feeling when he called. It was instant and it automatically brought back the memories of more than two years ago, and how raw her emotions still were. She made a lot of accomplishments in the past year here, but had a long ways to go to being recovered. At least she was no longer experiencing withdrawal symptoms from the drugs that had been given to her by Forester to control her. She swallowed hard. That had been a fear of hers, but her determination and strength to move on and be free got her through all of it and into recovery, physically and emotionally. She was still fearful though, and that would never change until Forester was dead.

"Hi, Sebastian," she answered.

"Hey beautiful, how are you?"

She smiled and leaned against the island in the large kitchen looking at the view through the sliders. "I'm well, and keeping busy."

"I hear you're really busy and haven't gotten together with your aunt and uncle for over a month."

She sighed. "I'm good, Sebastian. It's hard, that's all."

"Hard how?" he asked. He was always so easy to talk to, and she trusted him.

"As soon as I start feeling pretty comfortable and confident, I get that sensation like something is wrong and this life, the safety, is going to disappear."

"It's understandable, North. It truly hasn't been that long since everything happened. You've forced yourself to make things happen in record time. You've made great friends, established a career, and are moving on with your life."

"Not quite moving on."

"No one said not to date."

"I'm not interested in dating."

"Sure you aren't. You're a beautiful, classy, professional young woman. I know the guys swarm you."

"Oh really, how do you know that?"

"My uncle and aunt tell me."

"Your uncle and aunt tried to sneakily set me up with a guy they know."

He laughed. "I heard, and I told them not to do that, besides that guy was all wrong for you."

"Why is that?"

"He works for the bureau and drug enforcement agency."

She laughed. "What were they thinking?"

He laughed, too. "Are you in need of anything?"

"No. I'm doing good, Sebastian. What about you? How is the investigation going?"

"Nothing has changed. It seems that the focus is going toward bigger fish, which is what we expected."

Her belly quivered and she felt that fear simmering low. Her silence gave away that fear to Sebastian.

"I know, sweetie. You can't live your life looking over your shoulder. All I can give you as reassurance about Forester, is that he hasn't been seen in the United States. He is no longer the focus in the investigation, however, if he steps foot in the United States, I'll know and he won't be getting around without agents following him."

"I sure do hope so. If he did somehow get here and find me, he more than likely would kill me."

"Not from what we gathered at his home, and the intel on searches for you, and those attempts by men to get into the hospital."

"Don't remind me."

"Sorry, but we both know staying diligent is important."

"I'll never feel safe again, Sebastian. I know that."

"How about the counseling? Is that working talking with Ice?"

She was quiet. She had seen him only a few times and he was always checking up on her. When they did see one another, she made the conversation general and fought counseling.

"North, you like Ice. You can trust him. You're the only civilian he is willing to see. He deals with military only and he is my cousin."

"I know. I know, it's just hard to tell him things."

"Why? He's a great therapist."

"He's so big and well, good looking and intimidating. I'm embarrassed to tell him deeper things."

"Don't be. He has your file and he can read between the lines. Besides, you shouldn't be embarrassed. You were the victim."

"It's easy to just label me a victim, and especially with a therapist. Maybe I don't want to think about it all. About Tyler, too."

"Understandable, but talking about it, getting out that anger toward your brother, can help in a lot of ways. He was the only male in your life who stood for something."

"He stood for nothing. He worried about himself. I realized too late. Geesh, forget about this, Sebastian. I'm fine. I have to be. There's no one to count on but me."

"Damn it. Listen, in a few weeks I'll try to get there to visit."

"I'm fine, really."

"Text me if you need anything, and I'll keep you posted."

"Okay, Sebastian. Take care." She ended the call and sighed as she leaned back.

She thought about Tyler, and that was someone she didn't want to think about. He introduced her to Forester, but had Forester seen her first, or was she part of some bigger deal to save Tyler's own ass? She felt sick, hurt, betrayed and so damn angry. How could she ever trust any man, any person fully ever again when her own brother sold her body, her soul, her life to another man? Seriously, this kind of shit is so twisted and despicable, no amount of counseling, of talking about it, expressing emotions over it is going to heal her and make her feel whole again.

She pushed off the counter, took a deep, yet unsteady breath and released it. Time to get back to work, back to reality, back to looking like she was happy and normal.

Chapter Two

Casey looked at Amelia, Afina, North, Kai, and April, and gave a small smile. She had noticed that Amelia was being awfully quiet, and every time one of the guys came over to talk to them, or someone came over to hit on Afina, North, and April, Amelia tightened up. Casey could understand Amelia's fears, and she had a feeling more was going on with her, but Amelia wasn't budging. Who was Casey to give advice about men? Her own boyfriend tricked her, lied to her and then tried to kill her and Kai as well. That was a nightmare and it had been embarrassing. Casey was staying clear of all men, too. She didn't trust them. Whenever a guy approached to talk to her, she interrogated him and he got turned off. She shouldn't even bother, but being here with her friends made her more comfortable.

"I need to use the ladies room. I'll be right back," North said, and got up from the table.

Casey caught Mike looking at North the second she got up. Then Phantom and Turner did, too, and the two guys they were talking with. Could Afina's brother be interested in North? North would turn them down, just like she turned down all men who asked her out. When they asked North why she didn't date, she said she was too busy making money to pay her bills and it had to be priority. Afina pushed like always and got some answers. Apparently, North had been in a bad relationship and the guy was abusive. They didn't know how bad, but it upset them all. Apparently, there were a lot of dicks out there ready to abuse and hurt a woman. Why couldn't each of them find good men who would love them, make them feel special, and could heal their hearts, their bodies and souls? Was that just wishful fantasy thinking on Casey's part? She didn't know as that pain in the pit of her stomach increased. It was always there, would be there for a long time, perhaps forever.

Then she noticed Turner rub his side and then shake his head and look kind of pissed. What was up with that?

"Hey, why are you being so quiet? Are you feeling okay?" Kai asked Casey.

She gave her a smile. "I'm fine, just noticing some things, and enjoying hanging out here and not feeling uncomfortable."

Kai gave a soft smile and her friends looked sympathetic. "Hey, it's been a few months. It will take some time and Ghost and Cosmo said you could use the bathroom in their office if you are uncomfortable in the hallway."

"I just won't go down there alone. Maybe grab a few guys with guns or something, " she said, and then forced a smile.

Kai hugged her arm. "We'll all go together," Kai suggested, and then they raised their glasses and clinked them together.

These ladies had become her closest friends, and Kai saved her life, so she owed her everything.

* * * *

"So you guys are seriously thinking about moving here with your brothers? When did this come about?" Mike asked Rodriguez just as Denver got up off the stool, smiling wide and reaching his hand out.

"We sure are, in fact this is our real estate agent," Rodriguez said just as Mike had turned to see who Denver greeted. His eyes widened as North came into view, smiling, and greeting Denver and Rodriguez hello.

"So you found the hottest spot in town?" she said.

"How did you guys meet North? I mean with all the agencies around here?" Mike asked.

He noticed Rodriguez had his hand on her lower back still as if protecting her from anyone passing by, or maybe from Mike and his team? What the hell? They knew North already. *We met her first*, the words popped into his head.

"Actually, she introduced herself to us. Denver and I were talking out loud about this one place near the beach," Rodriguez said.

"Well a block from it, but still a view and you can hear the water," Denver added, and she smiled.

"One look into these gorgeous green eyes and we were ready to let her lead us anywhere," Rodriguez flirted, and North gave him a half-amused expression.

"You guys are relentless. So how do you know Mike?" she asked.

"We worked together a few years back," Rodriguez said, and didn't take his eyes off of North.

It bothered Mike and made him feel jealous. He had no right to be jealous. She didn't belong to him. He hadn't made a move or anything, and Turner was still up in the air about work and didn't think having a girlfriend would be fair or even possible. Some missions sent them away for months. A woman as hot as North would have men hitting on her all the time. Worrying would drive him, Phantom, and Turner nuts.

"How did that showing go this afternoon in the million dollar house?" Denver asked her.

"Oh it went great. They made an offer and the seller accepted."

"Fantastic. Let us buy you a drink to celebrate," Rodriguez said, then asked what she wanted, and she told him coconut rum and cranberry juice.

"You here with friends?" Denver asked her.

She pointed over toward the table where Afina and the ladies were. They looked on and stared, smiling and checking out Rodriguez and Denver. Mike, Phantom, and Turner listened as Denver and Rodriguez continued to flirt with her, ask about meeting tomorrow to look at more houses, and maybe doing dinner together. He was losing his mind feeling so jealous. Then Rodriguez got a call and Mike slid his arm around North's waist and pulled her closer. She gasped, and turned toward him looking way up into his eyes. She was a gorgeous woman, with the most stunning green eyes that drew you in immediately. Her body was perfection and fit really nicely against him. Her hand was on his chest and the other on his shoulder as she looked up at him shocked, hell scared. She was fucking incredible.

"You be careful with them. They tend to be very flirty, they're older as well," he warned her. He hadn't meant to come across sounding so damn fatherly, but he heard it in his voice. She looked surprised by his move, and she was shaking. He felt it and squinted at her. Was she scared of him? "North?"

"I'm a big girl, Mike, thanks for the brotherly advice, but they're harmless," she said to him.

Phantom moved in behind her and then was right by her side. "That's what you think."

She stared at Phantom, and their gazes locked and neither looked away. Mike felt the attraction instantly. This was the closest he ever got to North and he liked it, was aroused with her between him and Phantom. Fuck, he wanted her, and it was instant. Where the hell did these feelings come from?

"So, North, what do you say? Dinner tomorrow after you show us some houses?" Denver asked, and she slid from Mike's arms, and gave Denver a smile.

"Actually, I have a dinner date in the evening, but we could grab lunch if you want to get an early start tomorrow around nine? I can set up viewings at a few of the houses that caught your eye."

Denver gave her a smile. "Plan on it. Maybe Rodriguez and I will impress you enough to cancel that dinner date and spend more time with us," he said, and winked.

She chuckled, but Mike now wondered who the hell she had a dinner date with. One look at Phantom and his very blank expression and he knew he was thinking the same thing. Maybe Mike could ask Afina and find out.

* * * *

North was relieved to be away from the men and back over to the table with friends. She was completely caught off guard by Rodriguez and Denver's flirtation that was worse than when she first met them, and completely confused by Mike's behavior. He seemed pissed off, and when she made up the lie about a dinner date, hoping to catch some breathing space, she hadn't expected Mike's expression or Phantom's for that matter. Phantom looked ready to kill.

Both men were quite intimidating in size and attitudes. Turner, who remained in the background for the most part, hadn't said a word but she felt his eyes on her all night. Then she kept thinking about what it felt like to be pressed up against Mike and Phantom close behind her. It was crazy, but it had been so long since she experienced something as simple as a hug. To have strong arms around her, someone she felt safe with, and someone who didn't want to hurt her or use her. She gulped and felt so emotional. A fucking hug? Was she that desperate and needy for an embrace that now she would harping on the feel of being in Mike's arms? Mike, six feet three, muscular, scruff along his face, dark brown eyes, short brown hair with an air of arrogance, confidence, superiority and capability. He was sexy. Good-looking, mysterious, and she had no idea what he even did for a living, just that he disappeared with his team, and she assumed they were some sort of military or something.

Then there was Phantom, dark, mysterious, angry all the time. It was intimidating to even stand near him, never mind have him so close that he sniffed her hair. She didn't imagine that, did she? Had he done that? Jesus, she was freaking out. She looked down at her hand and her fingers were shaking. She took a deep breath and released it and focused on her friends' conversation the best she could.

Over the last few weeks since Mike and the team returned from some job whatever it was they did, something with the military, they had been keeping eyes on her, a lot. At first, she thought it was because of Afina, and then the incident with Casey and Amelia and of course

Kai. But then they not only watched her, but started to make a point to talk to her and even touch her. Like just a little while ago as Mike pulled her to him, it was like he was trying to claim possession of her.

Her heart raced and her body reacted to the thought. She was shocked. She glanced back toward the bar as her friends continued to talk about shopping at a new boutique a town over and some beach activities tomorrow afternoon, but she looked for Mike, Phantom and Turner. Sure enough, they were clustered together and all three men caught her gaze. She immediately turned away, felt her face flush and then gulped. The last thing she needed was to gain their attention. With her friends being involved with men, dating, or ending relationships that weren't working out, she was the one who remained single. Afina asked why she turned down dates with such hot guys, and she lied and said that she had been in a long drawn out relationship with a guy back home, and it took so much out of her she wanted a break to regroup and find herself. That seemed to satisfy Afina. For now at least.

Chapter Three

"I sure hope you have a hell of a lot more than that," Sebastian asked his partner Henry Young.

"It's minor when you look at it quickly, but just hear me out, Sebastian, okay?"

Sebastian leaned back in the chair at the office to listen to Henry.

"Okay, so I get this call from my buddy in New York who works security at the casino. Says that some big shot is coming in and has the place jammed up with occupying the entire top floor and penthouse suites. Anyway, he's babbling about high rollers, prostitutes and whatnot, but then he mentions this entourage of South American men with money. The kicker, is his buddy he's talking to overhears a conversation about a meeting and a guy named Synista. He thinks it's a funny name, sort of gangster and odd."

Sebastian sat forward. "Synista as in Forester's main guy, well one of them?"

"Yeah, I'm thinking it has to be him."

"We need to know for sure."

Henry smiled. "And that is why you and I are going to check it out tonight. My buddy can get us in no problem, and we can see who these high rollers are and what they're up to."

"Let's do it," Sebastian said to him.

* * * *

"What?"

"I got something."

"Don't waste my time."

"I'm not. It looks like Loconto wants to make a deal."

Forester sat forward on the chair. He was lounging by poolside, watching the women in their bikinis swim or work on their tans. None of them compared to his woman.

"Does he want to meet, or send someone to negotiate terms?" he asked Synista.

"He wants to meet, and is ready to have me speak to one of his representatives here at the casino."

"Is it safe, Synista?"

"I believe so. I haven't caught sight of anyone. The men have been very careful and Loconto isn't here. He sent Puevez. You know he doesn't usually show his face."

"I know, and I don't blame him. This is a good deal though. One he can't pass up. Do we have everything in place if he wants to make a visit or send someone to the warehouses and facilities here?"

"Yes, he does, but let me sit with his guy and see what we can come up with. It's happening, Forester. The hard work, the years of planning, is starting to pay off."

"I know, my friend. It has been a long, hard road."

"Then why don't you sound even the least bit happy?"

"You know why, Synista."

Synista sighed. "I've got nothing on her. It's like she disappeared."

"She had help. Someone in the agency."

"I'm not sure, Forester, I mean wouldn't our people on the inside have been able to find out by now?"

"Not if those who hid her have really covered their tracks."

"They'll screw up."

"It's been two years. She could be anywhere and with anyone." He ground his teeth and stood up, walking toward the pool. One of the women was sitting there leaning back sunbathing. The anger pooled in his belly. He wanted North. He needed her.

"When they do, we'll be right there to grab her and get her back to you. I promise, Forester."

"I know you did. Keep me posted on the meeting."

"Will do."

He ended the call and gripped the brunette by her hair. He didn't have to say a word. She immediately got up and bowed her head to him.

"The bedroom. Now."

He watched her hurry through the open sliders and right toward the hallway. His guards took in the sight of her body, thin, sexy, she would do for what he craved. To release this anger, and to possess something, pretending it was North. He walked to the closet and looked at the assortment of gadgets. He reached for the long leather strap, his mind on North and the last time he saw her. She was battered and bruised, begging for mercy. He longed to feel her underneath him. Hear her cry out his name and know that she belonged to him and only him. She better not be with any other man. If she was, and Synista found her that way, he would give the order to kill.

The thought enraged him and he stepped closer to the bed, and grabbed the brunette by her ankle and then flipped her onto her belly. She gasped.

"No other men. Ever."

He slammed the leather whip down and lost control. He was insane with jealousy, with need to have North here with him. He needed her, and anyone who stood in the way would die.

* * * *

"I got something for you."

"Oh yeah, what?" Synista asked.

"The agents who took North. I know who they are. Can watch them, and maybe find out where she is."

"Are you fucking lying? He won't be pleased if this is a fucking game."

"Not a game. I'm here. I see and hear shit. Haven't I kept you and the others warned about investigations, and surveillance?"

"What do you want?"

"What do you think? You know the account number. Pay what you think I should get for this. I'll send you what I have."

Synista ended the call and leaned back in his chair. He listened to Puevez talking to some of the men and they were preparing to head down to the casinos to gamble. This was a good day, would be a successful business venture for Forester and Loconto. He wouldn't call Forster to tell him about this latest call. He'd look at the information the agent sent to him and then decide what to pay. He wouldn't get Forester's hope up that North could be found. It would make his boss insane and he would do anything, even take risks that could destroy his empire to find her and have her back. Synista had to make sure the information was legit. When they did locate North, his boss was going to be a madman until she was in his arms and in his bed once again.

* * * *

"I like it. I think my brothers will, too," Rodriguez said, and gave North a wink. Rodriguez stood by the patio and looked toward the back yard and the ocean in the distance. They were a block from the beach, but from the deck they had a clear view of the ocean.

"Are they planning a visit to see it?" she asked.

"They're busy with work, but put Rodriguez and I in charge of this. It's been years in the making. I know they're going to love this town and the people," Rodriguez said, and eyed her over. He was totally flirting. The two of them had been all morning. She was grateful she made the excuse about a dinner date. Not that it was a total lie as of an hour ago when Uncle Billy and Aunt Stella invited her to their house.

"It's a great town, and you already know people like Mike, Phantom, and Turner," she said to him.

"What's the deal with them and you?" Denver asked, surprising her.

She squinted. "What do you mean?"

"Mike seemed pissed that we were spending time with you, and at the end of the night he pretty much threatened us."

"What?" she asked, feeling shocked.

"Yup, said to be respectful and a few other things. So we were wondering if that feeling for them is mutual," Denver asked.

She felt nervous and suddenly had a pain in her stomach, but she was used to deflecting everything away from her and especially emotions. She gave a soft smile. "I'll be honest with you guys. I don't date. I'm not interested in dating, and I'm just trying to live my life one day at a time, ya know?"

Rodriguez tilted his head. "Some dick hurt you?" he asked.

"Something like that."

Denver reached out and caressed her arm. She froze, and then reacted, and instantly pulled back.

"We should see the place one more time, and if you want I can send a link you can send your brothers to look things over." They didn't push and she was relieved as they locked up the doors and looked around before heading out to the cars.

"What about that dinner date you have?" Denver asked, sounding suspicious.

"It's with my aunt and uncle," she said, and then reached her hand out.

"So let me know if there's anything else you want to see again, and if you have any questions."

"Okay. Sounds good. Maybe we can check some of the other places next week that are on the outskirts of town where it's more quiet?" Rodriguez suggested.

"Sure thing, and they have a little more property, too. I know you mentioned that your brothers would prefer their privacy and no close neighbors. You may have to give up an ocean view."

"Or opt for beach front," Denver said, and winked.

She smiled, shook their hands, and headed to her car as they headed to theirs.

As she got behind the wheel, she thought about what Mike had said to them. With thoughts of him came thoughts of Phantom and Turner. She really didn't need that kind of situation that was for sure. North found them attractive. Who wouldn't? They were good-looking, in great physical condition, and also had a look in their eyes that was unique. It was hard to describe, but they didn't show emotion, where a lot of people totally did in their eyes. It had taken her a long time to try and not show her emotions. When she first arrived in Mercy things were tough. She got emotional, would just cry from a thought or freak out and lock herself in her car, or in her bedroom because she thought Forester had found her.

She knew it was better to just remain single and not even think about pretending her life was normal and she was free. She knew better. Sure, coming to Mercy had been a life saver, and changer, for the time being. It gave her an opportunity to have a professional career in something she loved, and even be around a lot of people and socialize and talk. She hated not talking, being alone with her thoughts, heck, just alone period.

Her mind went back to the three mysterious men. Men who disappeared because they worked for the government or military, or something. She didn't even know. Afina didn't seem to know either and made comments about not asking questions and that whatever they did was dangerous at times.

North gripped the steering wheel tighter and took a deep breath then exhaled. She didn't like the sound of that. There was already enough drama, danger, violence in her life, surely she didn't need to add in an attraction to such men.

"What am I thinking? God, not, no don't start wanting things you can't have, North," she said aloud, and then exhaled.

She pulled into the little bakery shop. She wanted to grab some cookies or something for Uncle Billy and Aunt Stella's house. As she got out, then hit the lock button she glanced around her, always trying to remember to remain on alert. It was natural. Sebastian taught her a lot of things as she recovered from her injuries. She knew how to shoot a gun, how to use a few self-defense moves, but in all honesty, she knew if she ever came face to face with Forester again she would freeze up and cower. She was deathly afraid of the man. He haunted her dreams at night. Sometimes she even felt his hands on her, and even his strikes. What got her the most, and what really freaked her out, was when she heard his voice, his words of possession and promise that no other man would ever have her body.

She gulped and looked around the café trying to decide what to get. She looked at the key lime pie, a favorite of Uncle Billy's.

"Can I help you?" the woman asked.

"Sure thing, I'll take the key lime pie please."

"Great choice." She heard the deep voice and turned around to see Turner standing there. He was holding a to-go cup. This place was known for their fresh squeezed lemonade.

Her lips parted and she tilted her head back to lock gazes with his eyes. "Oh, hi, Turner. How are you?" she asked. He licked his lower lip and eyed her over. She was glad she wore something nice and was in work attire. She could handle men better when she was in her professional mode. The flare beige skirt and the sleeveless silk tank in turquoise made her green eyes stand out.

"Not bad. What are you up to?" he asked.

The woman interrupted to tell her the price of the pie. "Excuse me a moment," North said, and fumbled with her purse in her bag.

Turner instantly made her nervous, especially because of her thoughts while driving over here. She paid for the pie and took the box that was tied with bakery string and looked back at Turner. The man looked lethal, and also tired. His dark brown eyes looked a little sunken in, or like he had shadows around them from lack of sleep. He wore a hat down low to his eyebrows that just added to the mystery and darkness of the man. Throw in the beard, the bulging muscles stretching out the material of the dark green shirt, and she had to take a step to the side. She bumped into another customer, and Turner slid his hand to her waist and pulled her closer.

"Be careful," he said, and she nodded like some mute. The man intimidated her. She tried to laugh off her fear, and the emotions she felt having Turner touch her.

He followed her outside. "So who is the pie for?"

"My dinner date," she replied, and then wondered why she wanted him to think she was involved with someone. Maybe because it would make things easier?

"Lucky guy," he said, and looked her over again, and somehow she felt it. Like he had the ability to touch her just with his eyes.

The way he looked at her unnerved North and she found herself blabbing to him. "Uncle Billy loves key lime pie. I know him and Aunt Stella will love it for dessert tonight after dinner. So what are you up to? Just strolling the streets?" she asked, trying to change the subject, and now felt like an idiot for revealing the truth. She didn't know why she reacted to this man this way. To Turner, Mike, and Phantom. God, Phantom was ten times harder to talk to than Turner. Mike was the easiest one to talk to. *Stop thinking*, she said to herself.

Turner squinted at her as he stood by her car. She looked way up at him. The man made his presence known. She felt it everywhere, even in places that should be numb from abuse. She gripped the pie box so tight she felt it cave in a little.

"Your dinner date is with your aunt and uncle?"

She swallowed and nodded, then unlocked the car and opened the door to put the pie on the passenger seat.

"That's where I'm headed now."

"You finish up with Rodriguez and Denver?" he asked.

"Just a little while ago. Boy are those two characters," she said to him and smirked.

He stepped closer and she bumped against the car. His hand went to her cheek and he gently pushed a strand of her blonde hair away from her face, then brushed her skin with the pad of this thumb. Her breathing hitched.

"You be careful around them. They get too pushy, or make you feel uncomfortable, you tell me, and I'll handle them."

She was caught staring at his face, and those eyes, so serious and cold. "I think they're harmless," she said, and he shook his head slowly then eyed over her top and then back to her lips. She was well endowed and she knew no matter what she wore, men looked at her breasts, their eyes focusing more on them than her. But Turner just glanced down and then back to her lips and her eyes.

"It's more than that. They're interested in you."

He was so close to her, she felt claustrophobic, turned on, aroused but also scared. "I'm not interested in them and I made that clear, Turner. So I don't need a big brother watching out for me." She went to move but his hand went to her waist and she gasped at the sensations.

"No need for attitude, number one. And number two, I'm not your big brother." Again, he looked her over. "The last fucking thing I want to be to you is a big brother," he said, and she was shocked. He started pressing closer and she feared he might kiss her. In a panic, she pressed her hand against his chest, and felt the rock-solid muscle beneath her palms.

"Turner, don't," she said to him.

He licked his lower lip and stared down into her eyes. He was so big and wide and filled with muscles. She felt the attraction and damned her life, her scars and fears that ran deep inside of her. She knew she could never entertain an attraction.

"How about having lunch or dinner with me, Mike, and Phantom sometime soon? Tomorrow?"

She shook her head. He slid his hand around her waist and pressed closer. She was between the car and him and her pussy clenched, and her nipples hardened. She longed to feel the safety of a man's arms. A real man, not one treating her as a possession and obsession, and an object he could strike. Her injuries had been severe. Her recovery intense, and thank God she had no visible scars to show for that.

"I don't date, Turner."

"Why is that?" he asked, still holding her. She tried pushing him away in a lame attempt, but he held her securely, his palm almost over her ass. If she pressed toward him, she would feel more of that large, warm, masculine hand there. Did she want that? Could she do that just to feel his hand there a second?

"I just don't," she said, and stepped forward. His hand glided lower, and she felt Turner's palm over her ass, and a digit against the crack. She gasped.

"I feel it, too."

She shook her head and tears filled her eyes. "I can't, Turner."

He squinted at her and squeezed her to him. "Someone hurt you?" he said to her.

She closed her eyes and clenched them tight. She could do this. She could push him away, but then she felt his lips against hers. The lemonade container dropped and his other hand, cold from the lemonade, cupped her hair and neck as he plunged his tongue into her mouth. She was shocked, but accepting to his control, his possession of her lips until she felt his hard erection against her belly. She pulled back and he sensed her need to slow things down, but when he released her lips he was breathing just as heavy as she was. His mouth was against her neck, his fingers still in her hair, cupping her head, and his hand possessively over her ass keeping her snug against his front.

"Holy shit, North. There's no way you can deny these feelings. No way," he said to her, then pressed his lips softly against her neck.

She gripped him tight, shocked at her thoughts. At the burning need to hold on to feel him, a man, so muscular, capable, strong and enticing to continue to hug her. Was she so desperate for a connection, for an embrace, for a man's hold that she allowed this to happen? She lowered her eyes and turned, pulling away. He released her hair and head and slid his palm down her arm, caressing it. Now he had both hands on her hips.

"Look at me," he said in a tone that was all commanding and a man in charge. She immediately shivered, lips parted, and looked up. He squinted. "You're shaking."

She couldn't say a word.

"Holy fuck. Who was he?" Turner asked. She wondered how the hell he could be so perceptive and know that a man hurt her, made it so that she feared being this close to another man. That Forester could be out there hunting for her, and one day would find her. She couldn't do this. Couldn't allow Turner into her heart. He would get hurt, killed, oh God.

She pushed him away. "That can't happen again."

He grabbed her wrist and pulled her back into his arms. He cupped her cheek, and she leaned back waiting for the strike to come. But it didn't. Instead, Turner's hard, icy stare spoke volumes.

"I'm not him, whoever the fuck he is. I'm not him and neither are Mike and Phantom." He pressed his lips to hers and kissed her once again until she was limp in his arms. When he released her lips to breath, he then hugged her tight, pressing her against the car and encasing her body with his, like a shield of protection from anyone and anything.

"This cannot be ignored. We'll work it out. Together," he whispered, but she knew she wasn't going to work it out with him, with them. No, she needed to put up the walls and remember the danger she was in, the pain and the surgeries she went through to save her life, and the wrath of the one man, the monster who haunted her dreams and held the power of her life, her body, and soul in his hands, still.

* * * *

Turner's heart was racing. The emotions, the attraction he felt for North was so strong he acted and kissed her. She kissed him back and he had a thousand thoughts until he released her lips and she pulled away and it became obvious that she was scared. He knew immediately some dick hurt her. Was it an ex-boyfriend? How badly did he hurt her? Did he break her heart, destroy her trust in people, in men? Did he abuse her? What? He wanted answers and he knew when Mike and Phantom found out that they would want answers, too. He could see the walls go up. "Don't push me away. Not after that kiss. Sweetie, I want more, and Mike and Phantom want you, too."

She shook her head. "No, Turner. This shouldn't have happened. I don't want this. I don't want a ménage. I don't want lovers. I don't want to be used. I don't want the games. I don't need this, and I want to be left alone." She opened her car door and quickly got inside. She closed it and he looked at her. He placed his hands on the driver's side door frame of the open window.

"I want answers. I want to know who hurt you. Is he from around here? From back north?"

"No, Turner. I'm not discussing anything. I just want to be alone." He covered her arm and ran his hand to her hand where she gripped the steering wheel.

"That's not true. You kissed me back. You let go a moment and it felt right and perfect."

"It doesn't matter, Turner. Just forget that it happened. It will never happen again." She started the ignition and he slammed his hand down on the car.

"God damn it, North!" He raised his voice, he was so pissed off but then her eyes widened and instantly filled with tears. She looked before she pulled onto the road and headed out. He stood there, wanting to chase her, to demand she tell him who it was that hurt her so badly that she feared these emotions, feared Turner's touch and words about wanting more. He never felt this way before. He completely reacted because he took a chance. He let some vulnerability show and he wasn't pleased with North's reaction at all. He felt insane a moment and thought of his brothers. That was why a ménage would work so well for them. They fed off one another, trusted one another, and they needed to be together in order to keep control and not just react. They didn't do alone, they did together, a team, a family, one unit, together.

He was frustrated and annoyed and he pulled out his cell phone.

"Yo, what's up?"

"Fuck, you aren't going to believe this. Is Mike there?"

"What's wrong?" Phantom asked, in that serious hard tone. He would freak North out even more than Turner did.

"Is Mike there?"

"He's around, what is it?"

"North."

"Is she okay?"

"I kissed her."

"What?" Phantom asked, his tone hard even over the cell phone.

"I'm coming home."

"With North?"

"Alone," he said, and ended the call and exhaled. Any other woman and damn straight he would be taking her someplace to meet Phantom and Mike and have one hell of a time. Never to their place. They never brought a woman there. But North? Hell, If North accepted hanging out, that would be exactly where he'd bring her. He felt instantly obsessed. She tasted so good, felt incredible in his arms, and that body, holy fuck, she was built to please a man. Feminine, petite, well-endowed and such a great ass. She was totally aroused by his possessive hold, even as he trailed a finger down the crack of her ass to her pussy. That's what seemed to send her running. The intensity of the kiss, the intimacy and power of it. Who hurt her? Was the guy still bothering her or part of her life? What the hell happened? He got to his truck and headed home. A glance in the mirror and he saw his expression, his dark eyes, the bags under them from lack of sleep. He was suffering with nightmares again, his PTSD getting the better of him. Two years had passed, but it didn't matter. Even the missions in between hadn't. He still looked back, pondering over that day he could have died.

Maybe they were out of their minds feeling something for a woman as young as North. They had a good ten years on her. Maybe that added to her fears? He didn't know what the fuck to think. Maybe Phantom and Mike would know what to do next. His mind traveled into a thousand thoughts. Could the guy who hurt her still be bothering her? Like maybe Casey's situation or even Amelia's? Amelia was so scared and fearful. She was a victim of abuse and any man could tell she was shy and reserved now, and unapproachable. Could North be in danger? His heart pounded inside of his chest. He was losing his mind, overthinking everything. He needed to calm down. He needed his brothers. They would know what to do. They had to be careful and handle this the right way. North could be the one. Holy fucking shit, she could be ours. He was shocked at the speed and direction of his thoughts. He went from not wanting to show vulnerability and risk rejection, to pressing her up against her car and kissing her, and now thinking she was the woman of their dreams, and center to the ménage they knew eventually they would have. Now? North? Holy shit.

* * * *

"Calm down," Mike said to Turner as he paced the kitchen.

"Calm down? How the fuck can I calm down? I kissed North, felt her ass, her body against mine and I want more. She pushed me away, denied the attraction and was shaking with fear. Someone hurt her."

"Well, we knew that much from conversations she's had with Afina and her own admittance that she was in a long drawn out relationship. Maybe it was worse than she let on," Mike said.

"It would explain why she doesn't date. Why she turned down Rodriguez and Denver, too, basically laughed at them," Phantom added.

"This is serious, Mike, Phantom. You have to hold her in your arms and kiss her. She fits perfectly. She's classy, sexy, and holy fuck, I can still smell her perfume. I'm losing my mind. One fucking kiss and feeling her ass, and I want to go find her and make her talk to us."

"You can't do that. If she was in an abusive relationship, or experienced a bad relationship, then handling getting to know her needs to be done with caution and patience," Mike said.

"You didn't kiss her and feel her kissing back, never mind pressing that body against mine. I felt so possessive and protective. I can't stand to think of who might be hitting on her. We've seen the men at Corporal's flirt and try to pick her up. Something is here between us. I mentioned you two as well and she didn't freak out, she just shook and looked like she struggled with what to say. She's been hurt badly," Turner added.

"We need to make a decision here. Are we talking about something temporary, or are we talking about a commitment?" Mike asked.

"We don't know if this is a game by her. We know nothing about her. I think we should hold back," Phantom said.

"You're just scared. I get it. I was scared to show some vulnerability but I did and it was great with her."

"I don't know," Phantom said, and stood up.

Mike knew that Phantom was not the kind of person to show emotions, or to put his heart out there. He grew cold, distant, quiet over the years from their missions and from being a mercenary. Killing took the love, the compassion out of a man. Maybe North would be a positive influence on all of them.

"Let's slow things down and see what happens. We'll make a point of talking to North when we see her. Maybe take the opportunity to be gentle and not so forward," Mike said, and gave Turner a warning look.

"Yeah, see how long you two last being close to her, inhaling her shampoo, and feeling her close." Turner exhaled.

Mike nodded before he spoke

.

"Let's take our time. It sounds like that's exactly what North needs.

* * * *

"You're being awfully quiet. What's wrong?" Aunt Stella asked North.

They were sitting outside on the patio overlooking the pool. They already had dinner and were on dessert, and the sight of it brought back more emotions and feelings she didn't want to face. She ran her finger over the rim of the glass of red wine she sipped at all evening. Turner was one hell of a kisser, and also had a temper. She couldn't help but to be scared of him, and not knowing what he did for a living, and who he really was, just added to her anxieties. If she had asked more questions, followed her gut instincts, she wouldn't have wound up involved with Forester and been pulled under like she had been. She needed to be smarter, and in doing so that meant remaining single and alone.

"Okay, spit it out," Uncle Billy demanded.

She looked at him, and tears filled her eyes. His eyes widened.

"What happened?" he asked. She shook her head. She didn't show emotions anymore. Or at least tried not to or she would start sobbing like an idiot.

"It's been two years; do you think I will ever be free? Ever breathe easy and be able to let go and live? Enjoy life like normal people do?" she asked.

"You're not living a normal life? You have a career. You have us, family, you have friends and hang out and have come a long way," he said to her.

"No, I've forced myself to get here, and used my fears, my anger as motivation. That fear is the push in everything I do, but now it's the fear that stands in the way of truly being able to be normal."

"I don't understand," Uncle Billy said, and looked at his wife.

Aunt Stella exhaled. "Who is he?"

North locked gazes with her and squinted.

"A man? This is about a man?" Uncle Billy asked.

"Just be quiet and let North and I talk," Aunt Stella said.

"There isn't anything to talk about really. You both know as well as I do that I can't entertain these feelings. I can't risk letting down my guard, never mind am I going to put these men into danger like that."

"Wait, these men? As in more than one?" he asked.

"Oh yeah, I had a feeling something like this might happen. In fact, I was thinking a ménage relationship could be the best choice for you," Aunt Stella said, shocking North.

"What? How could you say that?"

"They are very common around Mercy, and in other towns like ours. There are a lot of great things to say about ménage relationships, and especially when a woman has gone through the trauma and violence you have gone through," Aunt Stella replied.

"Aunt Stella, I'm not entertaining anything." She looked away.

"Why not?" Uncle Billy asked.

"Did Sebastian explain things to you? I mean realistically explain?" They were both silent.

"You won't have to remain in hiding forever. Sebastian is doing everything he can. You should move on with your life and that includes dating. You want to feel and be normal, then date like your friends are doing," Stella said to her.

"I don't need a man in life, one to order me around, treat me like a possession and dominate."

"Not all men are like that," Billy said to her, but North thought about Turner. He would be possessive. He would dominate and be forceful in his demands, and maybe even strike her to get her to cooperate. She didn't know and since she couldn't be a hundred percent sure, she wasn't taking a chance. Then she thought about Phantom. She knew even less about him, and one look and she sensed he was capable. Of what she didn't know, and that would make her keep her distance as well.

"What exactly happened, and who are the men?" Stella asked.

She looked at her. "It doesn't matter. My decision is made, and it's the best thing to do right now. I'm not ready."

* * * *

"We need to do something, Billy. If she met someone, or men, and she's feeling this way, then it means she likes them," Stella said to Billy after North headed home.

"What can we do? You know as well as I do that she is stubborn and still healing. She won't even see Ice."

"That's it," Stella said, and picked up her cell phone.

"What are you doing?"

"Calling Ice. He'll help her."

"She won't see him. She hasn't gone there in weeks."

"She came here tonight and it has been over a month."

He exhaled. "Whatever. Go ahead and try."

"Ice, it's Stella. We have some pushing to do," she said to him, and Billy smirked. Stella would make sure that North would find happiness. The woman just needed a little shove.

Chapter Four

"Damn, I don't like this, Henry."

"Of course not, because you're worried about North, but only you and I know where she is. If Forester sent his guy Synista here to do some sort of deal with Castella, then we just got very lucky. We should notify the commanders and set up shop. Get video surveillance, monitor their every move and—"

"No. We can't do that. You and I both know that we can't take that chance. We need to keep this small. Only our men that we handpick and we do it on the down low."

Henry stared at him. "You're still thinking that Tyler wasn't the only crooked agent, aren't you?"

"I don't want to believe it, but can't you see all the same signs I'm seeing? There were just too many fuck ups. Product was moved under the organization's nose, it was like Castella and Ferlong had connections on the inside. Now we've been over this. Tyler wasn't exactly top of his graduating class. He was a smart ass, liked to use his credential to gain attention and was always looking for the jobs that would give him more hours to make money. He wanted what the dealers had, and he got played."

"I still can't figure out why the hell that dick involved his sister."

"To get one debt paid off only to have another one to someone more powerful than the first person. North deserves a life. She deserves to be free from this shit, and to heal."

"How is she doing, anyway? Any updates from Ice?"

"She isn't seeing him." Henry raised his eyebrow up in surprise.

"And you didn't order her to?"

He shook his head.

"Damn, Sebastian, I would be more than willing to take some time off and go help her, you know hold her hand and see her through this."

Sebastian wasn't shocked. Henry couldn't stop talking about how beautiful North was and so sweet. He had been just as affected by her injuries as Sebastian had been.

"Cool it. You know she would turn you down."

"Well, she needs to be rid of all this danger and fear. Let's do this your way. You choose who knows about this operation and who doesn't. Maybe we'll find our rat, and put all these scumbags away once and for all.

* * * *

"This is the third time you cancelled. What is going on with you, North?"

Afina was concerned. Either North was seeing someone, or something happened to make her stay clear of Corporal's bar and all their friends.

"Nothing is going on. I've been busy and by the time Friday comes I'm exhausted and the weekend is filled with appointments. I have an open house Saturday that I hadn't planned on."

"Are you sure? Because it seems to me like you're avoiding Corporal's."

"Not at all. Listen, I haven't even been able to call Amelia back yet today, and Kai wanted to get together for lunch, but I'm swamped. Maybe in another week or so things will lighten up."

"You need to make time for yourself or you're going to get burned out.

"Can you squeeze in lunch?"

"Not today."

"Well where is this open house Saturday, maybe I can stop by to see you and say hello. Don't worry, I won't interrupt if there are potential buyers."

North laughed. "April just said the same thing to me. It's actually a really nice place. You'll love it. I'll send the address. Just text me when you'll be arriving."

"Okay. Well, we'll miss you tonight at Corporal's."

"Have fun and see you Saturday maybe."

Afina couldn't stop the thoughts running through her head. Was it just coincidence that Mike, Turner, and Phantom were in bad moods the last week? Ever since those two guys Rodriguez and Denver were in town searching for a house and flirting with North, her cousins were irritable to say the least. Maybe they were jealous? Maybe they finally realized that they needed to make a move on North before some other guys moved in on her? Maybe one of them made a move and North panicked? She wondered and immediately called April.

They had known North for only about a year but the moment her cousins met North, they liked her, but they were going through something. She had a feeling the last several contracts they had with the government had been dangerous. Mike hinted about being in a hospital, and then tried to cover that up. They kept to themselves and as close as she felt she was to them, she knew they had secrets. Something was definitely going on here.

* * * *

North didn't want to be here. She didn't want to talk to Ice. She didn't want to hear his consoling words, and it was like nothing was going to ever heal her. She looked out across the field as the kids played and people ran along the running paths. She walked, taking the long way to this spot, a spot many times she just sat and tried to clear her head. Today she was dressed for a run, ready to force herself into an almost state of exhaustion to clear her head, and she knew she would need that run when she was done talking to Ice.

She turned to the right and then the left, waiting for him to appear. Ice was definitely not your typical therapist. He was hardcore, badass, tattoos and beard, killer eyes, killer instincts, and a capable man. A man who had the ability to get through to even the roughest, toughest soldiers. Afina knew him, but Afina didn't know that North knew Ice so well. It made her feel sort of guilty. Her made up life here in Mercy was based on lies, except for her recent accomplishments. She was doing so well in the real estate business, moving up quickly, getting closer to being the top seller for the agency, and she loved it. Loved this town, these people, the patriotic atmosphere and even Corporal's which she had been avoiding like crazy. She was going to have to face her friends and face Turner, Mike, and Phantom again. God, she let Turner kiss her. What an idiot.

She spotted Ice as he walked around the path straight toward her. Sure enough he was on the phone as he walked, dressed casually like he was going for a run in sweats, a tight fitting t-shirt that showed off all his muscles and some of his tattoos. He was burly, intense, but when he spoke, he spoke calmly and compassionately. She wondered why he was single. Any woman would love a man so masculine and yet empathetic and caring. She was surprised by her thoughts. It wasn't like she was attracted to Ice, but now that Turner had kissed her the way he did, she was feeling things she submerged for so long. She thought they didn't work and that compassion wasn't needed in her life. That a hug could mean so much.

She tightened up. This was the wrong state to be in with Ice. He would draw out these emotions. He would make her talk them through with him and try to make her feel. She didn't want to feel. She wanted to remain numb to everything. It was easier that way.

"Hey, beautiful," he said, putting away his cell phone. She stood up and he hugged her and gave her a kiss on the cheek and she quickly pulled back, looked away and then sat. When she looked up, he was squinting at her. "Did you run yet?"

"Nope."

"Why not?"

"Figured I would need it afterwards," she said, and she heard the coldness in her tone.

He slid his arm over the back of the bench and shifted his body toward her as he crossed his leg over his other leg.

"So what happened?" he asked, straight out, no bullshit.

"Nothing happe—"

He shook his head, giving her that stern expression that stopped the words coming from her lips. She clasped her hands on her lap and thought of a bunch of things, and about Turner kissing her, his dominance and his anger when she stopped things.

"Someone got under that guard of yours, huh?" he asked.

She turned toward him.

He gave a small grin.

"I can handle this, Ice."

"By distancing yourself? By ignoring the pull to be human and to feel again when you've conditioned yourself not to feel?" he asked. He summed it up. Son of a bitch. Tears filled her eyes.

"I don't want to feel. I don't want to be vulnerable. I don't want to hurt. I can't take the emotions, Ice. It's so much easier to just be alone and to not have to feel for anyone."

"To be a robot? To work, to be in a routine and to be completely alone, lonely, sad, and scared?" he asked her.

"Fear is an everyday emotion I'm used to."

"There can be a difference between living your life in fear and living your life on guard, aware, and having a plan in motion."

"I do have a plan in motion. I actually have several of them."

"So you're prepared. That was something that concerned you months ago. Maybe this town, your friends, have helped you to feel more confident and to let down your guard a little."

"I let down my guard and that was when things changed."

"How so?"

"You want me to talk to you about it, but it's enough that I can't get it out of my head. I know the reality of this situation and the negatives have to outweigh the positives."

"What are the negatives?"

"When he comes for me. When he finds me and anyone close to me, anyone he perceives as a threat will die. That negative enough for you, Ice?"

He stared at her then placed his hand on her shoulder. "You're afraid for this man, for his life because by getting involved with you he could become a victim?" Ice asked.

"They could."

He squinted. "More than one man?"

She didn't say anything.

"What do they do for a living?"

"Don't even go there. First of all, I don't know. Something with the government. Right there a big no-no."

"How many?"

"Three?"

"You feel an attraction to all three?"

"One kissed me," she said, and her voice cracked and she felt emotional. He hugged her to his side.

"You have a right to be loved and cared for, North. You're young, beautiful and classy, have so much to offer."

She snorted. "So much to offer? Last time I checked a death sentence for getting involved with a woman wasn't at the top of the list of things guys want from a woman."

"North?"

She heard her name and both her and Ice looked up to see Phantom standing there. He had a hooded sweatshirt on over his head, his face slightly hidden and that darkness, that intensity about him appeared twofold.

She slid away from Ice and then looked at him, and he looked at Phantom, then at her before he stood up. When Ice did, she did.

"Good afternoon, Phantom. How's it going?" Ice said to him, and her heart hammered faster inside her chest. Ice put out his hand and Phantom shook it. He then looked at her, giving her the evil eye. Would Phantom think her and Ice were an item? Was he pissed because Turner probably went home and told him what happened between them? Shit.

"Out for a run?" she asked, trying to pull away from the awkwardness of this situation. Phantom stared down at her. He was tall, over six feet three, and had big thick muscles against the snug fitting hoodie.

"How do you know Ice?" he asked, and she looked at Ice.

"We've known one another for a while. I was just out walking and we bumped into one another. In fact, I should let you get back to your run, North. I know how much you enjoy that. We'll talk later in the week and I can give that contact information on my friend who is looking for a condo to rent."

Ice was helping her by making this story up and she was grateful. If Phantom knew Ice, then Ice knew what he did for a living.

"Thanks again and I'll talk to you later," she said, and he winked.

He looked at Phantom. "Good seeing you. Tell Mike and Turner I said hello," Ice said, and then walked away.

She swallowed hard, even the mention of Turner's name had her feeling hot and affected. Phantom looked her over. She wore a pair of spandex shorts, a tank top with a light long sleeve windbreaker over it. "Going for a run?" he asked, and she nodded.

"I'm doing the same," he said, and held her gaze.

She had to look away from him. Phantom was too intense, too dark, mysterious and unnerving to her. She always stayed clear of him, but then she felt his hand on her hip and she gasped and looked back at him. "Don't be afraid of me."

"I'm not," she snapped at him, and he licked his lower lip.

He stroked her hip. "You're shaking. I can feel it."

"Too much coffee," she lied.

"I don't like liars," he said to her, and squeezed her hip. She pulled away and bent down to tie her sneakers, which were already tied but she panicked. She felt too much. That attraction and that need.

"I need to get going," she said, and started to run. She felt him following her, and a glance over her shoulder and she knew he was looking at her body, watching her. He didn't stop or change directions. He kept up with her and she started to go through some of the other trails hoping he would get tired and slow down, but he didn't. Soon he was side by side with her but she was leading the way. She didn't know how, but she felt comfortable with Phantom by her side, despite how cold and distant he seemed to her. When they came toward the end of a path by the water that led through a wooded area, she hadn't expected him to grab her around the waist, lift her up and stop her. She gasped as he wrapped her up in his arms and pressed her against the tree and held her gaze. "Enough of the games." He pressed his mouth to hers.

She was shocked. Turned on, completely aroused by his dominance and his take control attitude. For a quiet, scary sort of man he was a complete turn on. She couldn't think as he plunged his tongue into her mouth in exploration as his hand slid up her waist to her breast and cupped it. She moaned into his mouth. Thank God they were alone on this path or they would be giving quite the show. She was overheated, perspiring, but she could smell his cologne combined with her body spray and prayed she didn't smell badly.

Their lips parted to breathe and he hugged her to him and she exhaled, her voice coming out like a squeak because his kisses and hugs were so effective she felt the tears emerge. He pulled back, cupped her cheeks, and gazed into her teary eyes, squinting.

"Tears?" he asked.

She gulped and tilted her head back against the tree. "This is bad. This can't be happening." She felt his lips against her neck gently spreading kisses.

"It is real. It's happening."

She tilted forward and shook her head. She reached up and stroked his cheek, felt the gruff beneath her fingertips. "I'm sorry, Phantom, I can't do this."

He growled low and pressed her firmer against the tree and his hard, solid body. "It's too late. I've tasted these lips. Felt this body in my hands." He slid his hand along her hip and to her ass. He pulled her against him and rocked his hips then kissed her again. It was wild as they battled for control of that kiss, and then in order to breathe, he pulled from her lips and suckled against her neck. She gripped his arms, he was so big, so hard like stone beneath her fingertips. She felt his tongue lick into her top and over part of her breast.

She tightened her hold. "Phantom. Oh God please don't do this to me. Please." She begged and tears fell.

He hugged her to him, kissed her neck and whispered into her ear. "Whatever it is, whatever you're so afraid of, we'll work it out. I'm not giving you up. This feels too fucking powerful. Turner will agree, and Mike, too."

"Oh God," she said, and then wondered what kind of lies could she tell them? How could she fight this and not allow it to happen? What could she do to stop wanting more?

He eased back and cupped her cheeks and saw the emotion in her eyes. "You're so goddamn beautiful." He covered her lips and kissed her again.

* * * *

Every instinct in Phantom's body went on alert. North had secrets. Seeing her speaking with Ice, a therapist he knew, made him wonder what happened to her, how badly she was hurt, and what could have possibly occurred in her life that she needed a man like Ice to talk to? His bullshit story of them knowing one another and wanting her help in real estate was a lie. He read people well. In his line of work no one could be trusted. Everyone was a threat and sometimes that paranoia flowed into his personal life as well. He didn't trust people. He hated having conversations in general never mind deep ones, but here he was walking alongside North and wanting more. Much more. Like her in his bed under him crying out his name as he made her come. It was instant and now he understood Turner's upset at her denial of the feelings and pushing him away when they kissed. Wait until they found out about today.

"What are your plans for the rest of the day?"

"I have work."

He gripped her hand stopping her from walking. He raised one of his eyebrows up at her.

"I do. It's an open house and then I have another appointment to show a few places to a client."

"Where's this open house?" he asked.

"Phantom, don't."

He stopped and pulled her close again and kept one hand on her hip and one he placed against her cheek. "Don't lie about how you feel. I'm the kind of guy to dissect emotions, I can tell you're scared. I want to know why, and is it because of me? Is it because Turner was so pissed you blew him off and walked away?"

She stared at him and he could see her expression change. "I don't like aggression. To be manhandled and made to feel like I could be struck."

"What? Turner would never raise a hand to you, neither would I, or Mike. He made you feel that way?"

She took a deep breath and exhaled. "I don't want to argue with you. This is what I was trying to avoid. I won't be some bedmate for the three of you. A convenient thing to do for now. I know there's an attraction but what would come of us? I only have a few good friends and Afina is one of them. Things get screwed up and my friendships will be over. I think it's wiser to remain friends."

"No," he said to her. She squinted at him. "You're lying."

She pushed from his hold. "I need space."

"You feel it."

"I didn't say I didn't feel it. I just can't entertain it. I'm sorry, Phantom, but there are things in my life, private circumstances that prohibit me from taking this chance, and getting involved with any man. I've never accepted a date, a fling or whatever, and I won't now. I just want to be left alone. Please."

He couldn't help but to be angry. To be offended in a way because he put himself out there. He took a chance at showing his emotions which wasn't something he was used to doing. "I took a chance, too, you know," he said to her, and then shook his head. He raised his hands up and stepped back. "I don't play games. Whatever, North. Whatever." He walked away.

* * * *

"This place is incredible," April said, then walked toward the sliding glass doors.

"It sure is. I would love to live here, but it's a bit out of my price range," Afina added.

North smiled as her friends walked through the place. She only had a few interested clients come through earlier.

"So you have like another hour or so right?" Afina asked, and leaned against the counter in the kitchen, sliding her palm along the dark granite countertops. It was an industrial kitchen that overlooked a large closed in patio with a pool and waterfalls. Past the yard was open land and then the ocean.

"I did have a client I was supposed to show some townhouses to, but he hasn't confirmed yet." She glanced at her cell phone.

"Well if he doesn't then you can meet us at Corporals' for dinner. We need to hang out and talk."

"Afina, it's been a long day."

"No! No more excuses. Now we don't know what happened and why you are refusing to hang out with us, but we're starting to get offended. What did we do wrong? Do you not want to be friends anymore?" Afina asked. One look at the others and North knew that they all felt the same way. She was screwing things up with her friends and she didn't want that to happen.

"No, of course I want to be friends. That's not it."

"Then what?" April asked.

"Yeah, what could possibly have happened that you refuse to come to Corporal's?" Kai asked. Amelia just stared at her.

She took a deep breath and released it. Sooner or later they were going to find out about Turner and Phantom. North winced just thinking about Mike seeing her and what he was going to do.

"Well?" Kai pushed.

"Turner kissed me," she said. They all gasped.

Afina reached out and grabbed her arm. "Mike, too?" she asked.

"Not yet, but Phantom did."

"Holy shit, Phantom? Jesus woman," Amelia said and started to pace.

"This is intense. No wonder you've been in hiding. Holy shit, did you sleep with them?" April asked.

"No, no of course not. It happened at separate times and it was out of my control. I mean Turner had me cornered then pressed up against my car outside of the bakery and suddenly he's kissing me and then I'm denying it happened and telling him it won't happen again. Then I'm in the park and Phantom appears, and then next thing I know he's running with me and we're down the path in the woods and he grabs me, presses me up against the tree and we're making out like teenagers. His mouth is everywhere and I'm totally confused and freaking out and then pushing him away, and Jesus, who the hell knows what Mike might do when he sees me. I can't allow this to happen. I don't want it to happen. I need to be alone. I'm good alone." She rambled on and her friends stared at her and then started laughing.

"Holy shit you're hot for them," Afina said.

"Well obviously she is. Look how red she is, and they're hot guys. Mysterious, too, we don't even know what they do for a living. Do you, Afina?" April asked her.

"Nope, just know it can be dangerous at times," Afina said.

"I don't want this," North whispered.

"Why not? You never let any guys close enough to kiss you and look what happened. Obviously this is different," Kai said.

"I'm better alone. I can't explain it, but it's just better this way," North said, and once again tears filled her eyes.

"Okay, there's more you're not telling us," Afina said, and crossed her arms in front of her chest.

"She's right. I can totally sense that," Kai said.

"I'm not saying a word. God knows I'm the last one to give advice or to share my feelings when it comes to men. Cavanaugh still wants me back and I regret falling for him."

"Amelia, he's still bothering you?" North asked her. She nodded her head.

"We should talk to Zayn," Kai said to her.

"No, I don't want to talk to anyone about this. It will only enrage him more."

"She's right. Look what happened with Casey and her boyfriend," April said.

"Don't remind me about that. It's amazing that Selasi, Zayn, and Thermo even let me come here alone with you guys today," Kai said.

"Maybe one of them are out there right now with binoculars watching us," Afina teased.

The thought made North nervous and reminded her of the danger she was in, and that they all would be in being this close to her. She didn't know if Forester had men looking for her, and if they found her and were watching, waiting for an opportunity to strike. They would kill first then ask questions later. She couldn't reveal her past and the danger she could be in. She certainly couldn't drag Mike, Phantom, and Turner into this situation.

"Shit, it's really, really bad. What aren't you telling us, North?" Afina asked.

"Nothing. There's no need to discuss this any further. Nothing will happen between me and your cousins. Nothing," she said, and thank God the doorbell rang saving her from having to discuss things further. It was a couple with a kid looking to check out the open house.

"So we'll see you later at Corporal's. I'll call you," Afina said a few minutes later, and her friends hugged her goodbye and she exhaled, feeling relieved they left and didn't push for more information. It started to make her feel like this wall was going up with them too now. She wouldn't go to Corporal's. No way. It would only make matters worse.

* * * *

"I'm not sure about this. It could be a fucking game she's playing," Turner said to Mike.

Mike gripped the steering wheel of the SUV as Phantom remained silent. "This is bull shit, and if you're instincts are right, both of you, then she was hurt, and the fact she was talking to Ice, just makes that fact more intense and more serious. We know what he does for a living and the people he sees. Soldiers who have been through traumatic situations, men who have considered committing suicide, men dealing with PTSD, so you know as well as I do that this is serious."

"Then maybe we should respect her wishes," Phantom said.

"We can't stop thinking about her or talking about her. I think the whole forgetting about her is out of the question entirely," Mike said, and then pulled down the side street to the single house that sat there alone a block from the beach. It was stunning, upscale and he could tell it would be spectacular inside.

"What if she panics seeing us and thinks we're stalking her?" Turner said.

"We're grown men. We know what we want. She's young and afraid, and we discussed this. No matter what the situation, we're pursuing her, right?" he asked, turning off the ignition and seeing the open house sign and knowing it was the end of the time allotted for the open house. They got out and walked to the front door.

Mike rang the doorbell and a moment later when it opened she appeared. She looked shocked, then her face went flush and he took in the sight of her. A sleeveless cream-colored dress that hugged her figure, the top dipped a little low but not too low, and she wore strands of necklaces that accentuated her breasts and drew your eyes to them. Her hair was half up in some sexy style that exposed her neck on either side.

"Open house, right?" Turner said to her, and she swallowed hard.

"What are you doing here? I don't want any trouble."

Mike pressed past her. "I think you're beyond in trouble with us," he said, and the others walked in. She headed toward Mike, and Mike saw Turner lock the front door and the top lock, too.

"I don't need this. I said I wasn't interested in pursuing anything with you guys and—"

She gasped as Mike wrapped his arm around her waist and hauled her up against his chest. He stared into her eyes as she held onto his shoulders.

"We came to check out the open house. You're the agent showing it. So show it," he said, but didn't release her until he saw that desire in her eyes and knew she did want this, that she felt the attraction but something was holding her back. As he slowly released her and she swallowed hard, he let his palm glide along her ass. She paused, as if liking the feel of his hand there and he knew it. She wanted them. What was she running from?

She exhaled and then put space between her and them. She handed over a sheet that gave the specs as he followed her through the house, his brothers in tow.

As she gave them the tour and described the upscale décor, the special custom molding, and of course super gorgeous views, he watched her, admiring her professionalism, the classiness about her but also that youthfulness that reminded Mike about how much older he was. Perhaps she just was afraid of their experiences and also an ex-boyfriend who maybe broke her heart? It could be that simple, but their agent, soldier minds read deeper and created more of a situation than there actually was. When they wound up upstairs in a study that looked out over the back yard, the pool and the view, he stepped closer to her, slid his palm along her waist, and as she tried to turn out of his hold he brought her closer to him. In front of him with her back against his front. His arm snug around her waist, he lowered his mouth to her neck and inhaled. "You smell so good, and look incredible. Better than this view."

She held her hand over his arm and tilted her head to the right. "Please, Mike, it won't work."

"It is working already," he said, and kissed her neck.

She leaned back against him and he suckled her skin, slid his free hand to her arm and wrist and encased it. The hand that was around her waist slid along her ribs to her breast. "Mike," she said, and went to press forward but then Turner was there. He cupped her cheeks. "Oh God," she said, and he winked.

"You're incredible." He pressed his mouth to hers and kissed her. Mike slid the hand that cupped her breasts down lower while he rocked his hips against her ass. He slid his hand up under her dress and she moaned and tightened against Turner as Turner continued to kiss her.

"Let him. Open for us. We know you're wet and want to feel more," Phantom ordered, and she tightened and moaned louder into Turner's mouth.

Mike tapped her thigh. "Do it," he said against her ear and she did. She stepped slightly, giving Mike room to lift her dress and slide his fingers along her hip and panties, against her mound, sliding his fingers back and forth along the clean, smooth skin before he slid a finger into her cunt. Her ass pushed back and he rocked forward.

"So fucking wet. I knew it. She feels it, men. She knows only we can make her feel like this. Want us like we want her."

Turner released her lips and suckled against her neck. "Incredible."

Phantom moved closer. "I wonder how delicious she tastes," he said, and lowered to his knees. Her dress lifted higher and she went to grip Phantom, maybe to stop him, but Mike didn't want to frighten her by holding her wrist still, so he released it and she grabbed onto Phantom's shoulders, but Phantom was on a mission. A second later, her thigh was over phantom's shoulder and Mike pulled his fingers from her cunt and Phantom replaced them with his mouth.

Mike unzipped her dress and Turner slid her strap down on one side and leaned down to suckle her breast.

"Oh God please. Please, what are you doing to me?" she asked, and began to rock her hips.

"Loving you. Showing you how turned on you make us and how much we want you," Mike said, and gripped her neck under her hair, turning her slightly and kissing her. Phantom continued to stroke her cunt and feast on her. Turner was sucking her breasts and pulling on her nipples, and Mike was devouring her moans when she came. She pulled from Mike's mouth and gasped for breath.

"My turn," Mike said, and they shifted positions. Mike fell to his knees. Phantom slid up and wrapped an arm around her waist so she wouldn't stop this, and turned her face between his palms. "You're incredible. My dick is so fucking hard, baby. I want in," he said, and pressed his mouth to hers. She gripped onto him and Mike licked her cunt, tasted her cream, inhaled her scent with her sexy, toned thigh over his shoulder and her pussy in his face. He nipped her clit and she came again. He slid his fingers over the cream and then to her asshole. She jerked forward and Phantom rocked against her. At the same time, Mike slid his finger into her asshole and she cried out. Turner hugged her to him.

"Oh my God. Oh my God I never. Never." She moaned against his shoulder and then Turner lowered and Mike took his place.

He cupped her cheeks and stared into her glossy green eyes. "Taste yourself, baby. You're delicious." He kissed her hard on the mouth. She kissed him back but he was in control and then she jerked.

"Fucking delicious," Turner said.

"Her ass is sucking in my fingers. Holy fuck she is tight," Phantom said, and Mike stared into her eyes as she blinked, and he knew Turner was fingering her pussy while Phantom fingered her asshole.

"You feel it. You want it and you want us like we want you. Go with it, North. Whatever the fears we'll deal with them later. Let us make you feel good and you make us feel good. Come on, baby."

"Not here," she said.

"Why not? You're wet and ready. The open house is over. The doors all locked," Phantom said, and suckled against her neck as he continued to stroke her like Turner was.

"Right fucking here, where you look hot and it's spontaneous and no one will know," Mike said to her.

"It's naughty and dangerous and you're turned on by that. By us," Turner said, and released her. He stood up and undid his pants. She reached out, placing her hand against his chest.

"I can't," she said, tears filling her eyes. Mike felt like there was a vice grip around his heart.

Phantom pulled back too now and she fixed her dress. Phantom zipped up the side and she adjusted her breasts in it. She was emotional and Mike cupped her cheeks as Turner and Phantom stared at her now, too.

"It was that fucking bad, whatever the fuck happened to you, was that bad?" Turner asked her.

She nodded her head.

"Fuck," Mike said, and pulled her into his arms and hugged her. She cried as he glanced at Phantom, who looked ready to kill and then at Turner who was none the happier. North had a past and secrets, and they wanted her as their woman, in their bed, in their lives, so it was up to them to gain her trust and get her to reveal exactly what happened.

Chapter Five

Phantom drove in her car with her and she knew it was because they didn't trust her to follow them to Corporal's. It took a lot to talk them out of following her to her place. She mentioned that Afina and her friends expected her at Corporal's and since she was duffing out on them the last week, she needed to go. They were none the happier, especially Phantom.

He slid his palm along her thigh as she drove. She tightened up and inhaled, catching his cologne and remembering what it felt like to have his fingers and mouth on her cunt and then in her ass. She couldn't believe she let them finger her, and make her come in that house. Thank God they didn't have surveillance cameras.

"What are you thinking right now?" he asked her.

"That I'm glad that house didn't have surveillance cameras inside. At least that I know of." He squeezed her thigh. "You put a stop to it going any further, so if there are cameras you should be fine."

"Seriously, you think so? I nearly had sex in an open house."

"It would have been fucking hot, and guaranteed we would still be there, maybe bending you over that big jacuzzi tub."

She gripped the steering wheel. "What's with you talking so much suddenly?" she snapped at him.

He slid his palm higher up her thigh between her legs. "You, North. You do it to me," he said, and she was grateful they got to the parking lot of Corporals. She turned into a spot next to Mike's SUV and then turned off the engine. She went to move and Phantom cupped her cheek and drew her closer. "I know the walls are going up, and you'll deny what happened, so I need something to hold me off until later." He pressed his lips to hers and kissed her tenderly. The knock on the window made her jump, and Phantom pulled from her lips and exhaled.

"No patience," he said and got out.

She ran her fingers along her lips and grabbed her purse as Mike held the door open. Before she could move, Turner pulled her into his arms and kissed her again. He ran his hand over her ass and plunged his tongue deeply into her mouth. She wondered why they left the house. This was going to get worse and worse. He released her lips and Mike took his place. "One more kiss before you pretend you're not coming home with us tonight," he said, shocking her, and then his lips were over hers.

Mike held her hand as they walked into the place. She tried to pull away but he didn't allow it, nor did Turner and Phantom. They flocked around her and people noticed. Including her friends and of course Ghost and Cosmo, who owned the place and knew Uncle Billy.

Her friends greeted her but Mike kept her close and Afina looked on with excitement.

"What's going on here?" Afina asked.

"What does it look like?" Mike said very serious like, and North swallowed hard.

"North!" She heard her name and saw Rodriguez and Denver as they approached. They kissed her cheeks hello and hugged her and the whole feel of it was different. The atmosphere, the expressions on everyone's faces, and the scowl on Phantom, Turner, and Mike's faces.

"What's going on?" she asked.

"We need a picture with you. We have some friends who want to come down here to look for places, too, and we told them about you," he said, and then turned the camera on them. She smiled as they did a selfie with her. As she stepped back, they rambled on about things, but as Rodriguez placed his arm around her waist, Mike gripped her hand and pulled her closer. "If you don't mind, she's with us right now," Mike said.

Rodriguez and Denver eyed her over then Mike, Phantom, and Turner. "Fuck, I knew there was something between you four. That's awesome. She is one hell of a woman. No wonder she kept turning us down. This a secret or something?" he asked.

"It's new," Turner said.

"We aren't really dating, I mean we just started talking about it." Phantom pulled her into his arms and kissed her. She heard the chuckles and the congrats and high fives, and when Phantom released her lips he pulled her over toward a private table by the bar. She wouldn't dare look at her friends. She couldn't. She was overwhelmed. But Phantom held her in his arms and kept caressing her back and her ass as Turner and Mike stood just as close.

"You'll get used to it," Turner said, and kissed her bare arm.

She glanced way up at Phantom and those dark serious eyes. "Why did you do that?" she asked him.

He stroked her cheek. "They have had their eyes on this body, on you for weeks, and it has pissed me off. You're going to be mine and Mike's and Turner's and no other men are going to try and move in on what is ours."

"I didn't say I accepted anything."

"Baby, your kisses, your eyes, your body language and your responsiveness to our touches, speaks volumes. Now let's have a drink or two, and then call it a night. We've got some more exploring to do and plans to make," Phantom said, and caressed her cheek with his knuckles, giving her a wink.

* * * *

"Those guys are crazy. They're back looking at houses and now they're at some bar," Agent Morgan said to his buddies. He was part of the group chat they started. He and his brothers were thinking of looking for a vacation home and then eventually a place to move to in retirement.

"Damn, that's their real estate agent? She's fucking hot," one of the other agents said, and two others walked over.

"Let us see. Wow, I think I need to go down there to look, too." The guys started laughing.

"They said she is awesome and highly recommend her," Morgan said.

"Lucky bastards. If I went down south looking for a vacation home, I'd get some fat ugly chick with no personality. That woman could be a damn model," Agent Carton said.

They all started talking about the blonde.

* * * *

Sully Frame looked at the group text message and he couldn't believe it. His heart began to pound and he had to do a double take. All the guys were talking about the blonde real estate agent who was hot, and that Rodriguez and Denver were trying to get into bed with. He recognized her immediately. This was the break he had been waiting for. How the fuck did it all fall right into his lap? He had to remain calm and not give away any indication that he needed info.

"Hey, where are they looking?" he called out to the other agents.

"Ahh, get a good look of her, too, huh, Sully?" Morgan asked.

He gave a smile. "I'm into brunettes, but I have a cousin in Florence. Is it close to there?" he bullshitted. He didn't have family.

"Mercy, I think it was called." And then the guys continued to talk about North.

He walked away and down the hallway to a private area and he took a screenshot of the picture before he made the call.

"What do you have?" Castella asked.

"It's going to cost ya, but worth it," he said.

"Send it."

"Will do and I'll be in touch later." He ended the call and then sent the picture to him.

Castella had been searching for this woman for more than a year, maybe even two. The only agents who knew where she was were Sebastian and Henry, and they wouldn't budge or let anyone in on the info they had. They were still trying to catch Castella, Forester, and even Loconto. That wasn't going to happen. Not with him working both angles and getting paid as an informant for Forester and his buddies. Every potential mission or operation would self-destruct from the inside out and these guys like Sebastian and Henry would never figure out it was him. He had to hide his grin. Another few operations and he could call it quits and live off the money he made from doing this. He couldn't help but wonder why North, that blonde, was so important to Forester. Sure she was hot, had big breasts and looked like a model, but he could get any woman he wanted. What did she have? He wondered and then shrugged his shoulders. It didn't concern him. Money talked, and bullshit walked. He was going to be just as rich in no time at all.

* * * *

North loved the way it felt in their arms and having them close. As the night went on, everyone and everything around them disappeared and it was like it was only them and her together. She stared at Phantom. She was standing in front of him between his legs. Turner stood right behind her, his hand on her hip and Mike was on the other side.

She was avoiding their questions and Phantom was getting frustrated. She didn't want to talk. She didn't want to divulge anything to them, she just wanted to keep feeling. Why? Because she longed to be hugged, to be held and protected, and she felt protected in their arms.

"You're not saying a thing. We're trying here but you aren't," Phantom said to her.

She slid her hands up his chest and looked into his dark brown eyes. His expression was intimidating. The three of them had a presence about them that made her want to cower and hide or bow in obedience, and that made her hold out even more. She didn't want to feel like an object. She had taken so much abuse from Forester that she started to become numb to the strikes, to the commanding words, to his form of discipline. She clenched her eyes closed. His palm slid along her ass. "What is it?" he whispered, and she shook her head and pressed her cheek against his chest. His other hand caressed up her back to her head, cupping it. Her eyes landed on Turner.

"Why aren't you talking?"

"I don't want to talk, Turner. It feels good to be held like this. To be hugged. Let's leave it at that," she said, and gave Phantom a squeeze before she lifted her head up and away from his chest. His fingers were in her hair holding her, tilting her head up toward him.

"Are you ready to leave?"

She felt instantly upset. Did what she say turn them off? Make them want to end this? They were masculine men, authoritative, commanding, was she being sappy now and they didn't want that? She pulled back and his fingers slid from her hair and she grabbed her purse off the bar. Phantom grabbed her wrist. "What are you doing?"

"Leaving, like you said. I told you this wouldn't work. That I can't be with you guys and it's better for me to be alone. You didn't want to listen and now you're pushing me away when I let down my guard, so let's call it a night." She pulled her hand from his and then started walking away. Her friends were long gone. The tears and emotion had her choking on her own swallow. They got to her and made her feel things, and now they were pushing her away. She did this.

Phantom grabbed her around the waist and turned her toward him. Turner and Mike were right there with confused expressions on their faces. "What in God's name are you talking about? We aren't pushing you away. You said you didn't want to talk but were fine with feeling, with having us hold you. You felt safe. We want to be alone with you. Help you get more comfortable with us so you'll let us in." She was shocked, but then Phantom drew her back against his chest, his muscular arms encased her body and he kissed her head.

"You're driving me crazy. Come on," he said, and slid his hand to hers and then opened her door. She got in and he walked around to the passenger side. She didn't have to look to know that Mike and Turner followed them.

When they got to her apartment, she felt anxious and unsure of what would come of this. But when she thought about them leaving she felt empty and afraid. She tried to act casual as she invited them into the apartment and they were impressed with it all, including the view. Mike looked out on the balcony as the sound of the ocean filled the air. It was dark, but the moonlight was so bright it illuminated the beach and cascaded over the water.

"It's a beautiful night," she whispered, joining him. Turner and Phantom came out there, too.

"This is impressive," Turner said, and placed his hands on her hips. His lips pressed against her neck, and his beard tickled her skin. She moved her hands back over his hands and he slid his hands over her wrists, locking them in front of her. His body pressed her forward, and he held her hands with one hand against the railing in front of her. It was erotic and she felt sexy, needy for their touch.

"Relax and just feel," Turner whispered, kissing her ear, her neck, making her shiver as his whiskers brushed against her sensitive skin. Then she felt his palm slide along her waist, just as she felt his erection through his jeans press against her lower back. She looked to the left and Phantom held her gaze as Turner slid his palm under her dress, maneuvered under her panties and fingered her cunt.

"Oh." She moaned.

"Look at me," Phantom said firmly, and she widened her eyes, staring at him as he stepped closer and pressed a hand to her belly and used his other hand to maneuver into the top that gaped open, and he found her nipple. He pinched it, tugged on it, and the burning needy sensation hit her core.

"Are you on the pill?" Mike asked, coming on her other side and unzipping her dress.

"Yes."

"Do you want us, like we want you?" Turner asked, and stroked two fingers into her cunt a little faster as he rocked her hips, his cock against her ass and his one hand restrained her wrists over the railing. Did she want them? Was she willing to risk so much to continue to feel like this?

"Answer us. Yes or no?" Mike commanded.

"Yes," she said, and Turner released her wrists and pulled his fingers from her cunt as Phantom moved his hand from her breast, and Turner lifted her up into his arms and carried her back inside. She heard the balcony door close and lock and she hugged Turner, nuzzled against his neck as fear and confusion, filled her. Was this right? Should she warn them of the dangers that could lay ahead, or should she just see what happens? Maybe it wouldn't work out and no one would ever know about this night.

He lowered her feet to the floor in front of her bed. He reached for the hem of her dress and lifted it up and over her head.

His eyes were glued to her breasts, to her hip and belly. He grabbed her ass and pulled her against him. "You're incredible," he said to her and kissed her again. Mike moved in behind her and unclipped her bra, then ran his hands along her back.

Turner released her lips and her bra fell down her arms. She let it go and all three men stood there looking at her.

"Holy fuck, North. You're incredible. Jesus," Mike said and cupped one breast, lowered his mouth to it and began to feast on her. Phantom pulled off his shirt. Turner was almost completely naked and then Phantom slid his hand up her wrist and arm and lowered to take a taste of her other breast.

"Oh, oh that feels so good."

"Just wait," Turner said, and she locked gazes with him. With his muscular chest, dips and ridges of muscle all along his body, some scars along his skin and to his cock, thick, long and ready. She was going to do this. She was going to just feel. He stepped closer and put his hands on her hips and lowered her panties. She stepped from them as Mike and Phantom took her hands. Turner lifted her by her hips and pressed her onto the bed. Mike lifted one thigh and Phantom lifted the other so she was fully open to their ministrations.

"Oh God. Oh." She panted, shocked, uncertain of what they would do to her.

Mike licked her nipple. "Easy. Just feel," he said, and a moment later Turner's fingers were stroking her cunt, his mouth was exploring her mound and then her clit and pussy while Phantom and Mike feasted on her breasts and held her arms above her head.

She lifted her torso up. "Turner, oh, Turner." She moaned and came. When his tongue lapped over her asshole she shook and wiggled trying to get free.

"Easy, baby. Every part of you is going to belong to us. Every fucking hole," he said, and pressed his finger into her asshole then latched onto her cunt and played her body like a fiddle.

She wiggled and moaned and rocked her hips, feeling desperate for more. "She's ready, Turner. Come on," Mike said, and Turner pulled fingers from her ass, lifted his mouth from her cunt, and aligned his cock with her pussy. He held her gaze. "Want me?"

"Yes. Yes please." She begged and he nudged his way in. She moaned and could feel how thick and hard he was. "Oh."

"Open for him. Relax those muscles," Phantom demanded, and pinched her nipple. She felt her pussy cream and clench.

"That's it, baby. Let me in. You want us and we want you. It's perfect."

"It's been so long. Oh God," she said, and tried to submerge the memories of the past and what she thought about sex and the pain it caused, but as Turner Mike and Phantom plucked her nipples, suckled against her neck and were persistent with their ministrations, she relaxed those muscles and Turner thrust all the way into her cunt.

"Holy fuck," He exhaled, teeth clenched, and he didn't move. "My God. Fuck, you're tight," he said and started to pull out but then thrust back in. She rocked her hips and he countered. Before long they were both thrusting into one another as Mike and Phantom cheered them on.

"Look at you, you're incredible, woman. Look at those breasts. Fuck they're so big and full. I need another taste," Phantom said, and cupped her breast as Turner lifted up and gripped her hips, pulled her toward the edge of the bed more, and began to stroke into her faster.

Mike locked her wrists above her head and pecked at her lips, her neck and then her breast. "Ours. This body, every inch is ours.'

"Oh!" She cried out her release and Turner lost control. She was shaking so hard especially as Mike used his palm to move up and down her belly and over her pussy. Turner thrust faster, deeper, and then grunted as he came. He was panting for breath and leaned over her to kiss her. He gave her hip a tap and held her gaze as he gave the order. "Mike then Phantom. This is going to be one hell of a night."

He eased out and Mike was there to take his place. He lifted her up into his arms and she straddled his hips as he kissed her. She absorbed his control, his dominant ways, while he caressed her back and ass.

She kissed his mouth, plunged her tongue in deeply and ravished him as his hands explored her body possessively. He pressed her over the edge of the bed and aligned his cock with her cunt as she continued to kiss him. His large hand felt so sexy and arousing brushing against her inner thigh to align his cock with her cunt. She wanted him, wanted more. She never felt anything like this before. He started to ease the thick hard muscle into her pussy when she released his lips. He stood by the edge of the bed, gripped her hips and raised them up and began to thrust into her.

"Arms back. Hand over complete control to me, North," he commanded, and she gasped and cried out her release. He lifted her higher, held her gaze as he slid one hand from her hip to her breast and pinched the nipple. She was flowing like a faucet and he complained about not lasting. "Too fucking good, too tight. I can't hold back. You're so fucking hot, baby. Fuck," he said, and came. He lowered her down and kissed her hard on the mouth. She hugged her legs to him, but then Phantom was there. Mike winked at her, that sexy grin, whiskers along his handsome face and all those tan, hard muscles had her licking her lips. He eased out and got up and Phantom lifted her up into his arms. He hugged her tight, ran his palm along her ass, slid a finger down her crack and suckled against her neck.

"You're sexy, feminine, and a damn goddess. Where you been hiding these?" he asked, cupping her breast and lowering his mouth to it. He held her in his arms as if she were light as a feather. His hand plastered over her ass, keeping her in place. That expression on his face was so intriguing and yet scary. She ran her fingers through his hair and lifted high, letting him reach her breast with his mouth, but then as he suckled, his fingers slid into her pussy under her and she lifted up and down riding his digit. He lowered her to the bed, his mouth feasting on her cunt as he spread her wider and then licked along her body. "Arm up," he ordered, and she slowly raised her arms up, felt the cool air against her pussy and ass as they were laying over the edge of the bed. She held his gaze as Phantom slid his palms up her arm to her fingers, entwined them and then pressed his mouth to hers. He kissed her gingerly and she tilted her torso up, wanting, needing his cock to fill her up, too. He released her hands and slid lower, taking a breast into his mouth as much as he could fit, first the left then the right. He trailed his tongue down her cleavage to her belly, pressing into her belly button and then swirling his tongue along her hip bone on the right then the left. She was panting.

"Please, Phantom, please," she whispered. His brothers watched, licking their lips and then following his mouth with their eyes. His tongue delved into her cunt and she gasped.

"Hands up," Mike ordered. She glanced at him, at that commanding expression and then at Turner. She lost her mind. Whatever they wanted she would give them. His tongue slid along her cunt then over her asshole. He lowered, spread her thighs and then licked back and forth over cunt and asshole.

"Oh God please. Please do something."

"I am. I'm getting you ready for the three of us," he said, and her eyes popped open as his finger slid into her asshole.

"It burns, oh, oh, Phantom."

"It will ease as we get it ready."

Mike cupped her cheek. "Ever have a cock in your ass?"

"No.

"Oh boy, that's it, Phantom," Turner said, and then licked his lips and stared at her body.

She felt Phantom lift up and then his cock was at her entrance. "First time like this," he said, and slid into her cunt. She gasped at the tightness, and then girth of his cock. He shoved all the way in.

"Fuck yeah," he said, and thrust again and again as she panted and rolled her head side to side. It was so hard keeping her arms above her head.

"You trust us? You want all of us as we want all of you?" he asked.

"Oh yes, yes, Phantom. Please." She begged and she didn't even know what for. He pulled out, flipped her onto her belly, had her feet on the floor, her torso and chest to the bed, and he lowered down and licked her again from cunt to anus. He slid a finger into her ass and her entire body responded. "Yes, oh, Phantom. Oh please."

"I know, baby, I'm going to help ease that need right now."

She felt him pull his cock out of her cunt and then it was pressing against her puckered hole. "I got something for her, too," Turner said, holding his cock in his hand. She looked at it, and then Phantom pushed into her asshole.

"Oh!" She moaned and he grunted.

"Holy fuck. Let's do this. She's ours. I'm never letting her go. Not ever," he said, shocking her. But she felt it, too, and he eased her up and Mike lay on his back, his legs over the edge of the bed and she lifted with their help, and with Phantom's cock in her ass and then she eased her pussy over Mike's cock. Tears stung her eyes. She felt so much.

"Holy God, baby, it's incredible. You're incredible," Mike said, and kissed her.

"Come here," Turner said, and slid his fingers into her hair and she knew what he wanted. She knew what a ménage entailed and tonight she was throwing inhibition and fear to the wind and letting go big time. Anal sex? Holy shit. She eased her mouth over Turner's cock and began to feast on him. Hands smoothed along her ass and hips, then her breasts as both Mike and Phantom thrust into her body. She moaned and felt more cream release and then Phantom cursed.

"I'm there. Fuck, I'm there," he said, and then thrust hard and deep four more times in her ass before he came.

"This mouth. Sweetie, you're perfection. I can't hold back. If you don't want to swallow me, release me," he said, giving her the option.

She gripped his thigh and sucked as he came. When he pulled out, he was panting for breath and then Mike rolled her to her back and thrust into her several more times before he came. He fell against her body, breathing against her neck and ear.

"Amazing. Never like this, North. Thank you for trusting us," he said and then kissed her.

* * * *

They eased onto the bed and Mike held her in his arms. Phantom got washed up, looking around her bathroom, noticing the upscale décor, the marble and the big jacuzzi bathtub. There were candles all different sizes that were lit at one point or another. He could imagine North laying in a bubble bath, bubbles up to her breasts. He licked his lips. Her body was phenomenal. She was thin, toned from running, but well-endowed and that ass, holy fuck, she let them make love to her together. His heart felt like there was something squeezing it. His gut instincts in tune to the reality of this relationship if it were to progress. He wanted it to. He knew instantly he did, but what about North? What was she holding back? They would need to ease it out of her, yet part of him was concerned to know how bad it was. He joined them in the bedroom. Mike was holding North in his arms and she was pulling the blanket up to cover her body.

"No need for that. We're just taking a little rest before we do it all again," Turner said, and slid along the bed when he stopped short, his hand under the pillow next to Mike's he rested on.

"What the fuck?" Turner pulled out a gun, a Glock.

North sat up. So did Mike.

"A gun under your pillow?" Turner asked, holding it. He checked it.

"Loaded?" Phantom asked.

"And ready to go," Turner said.

"Give it to me," she said to him, putting her hand out.

"Why do you have a gun under your bed?" Mike asked, sliding his palm up her hip. She took the gun from Turner, checked the safety and then climbed over Mike and put it into the drawer by the bed. She then walked to the closet door and pulled down a robe, got into it, breasts moving with her motion, making Phantom instantly want her again, but this gun thing added to his concerns.

"Come here, North," Mike said to her, as he sat on the edge of the side of the bed, legs open, still naked. Turner stepped into his jeans and so did Phantom. Neither man buttoned them up. She walked to Mike, ran her fingers through her blonde hair and he gripped her hips.

"Why the gun under your pillow?"

She swallowed. "Safety, security at night when I'm here alone."

Turner walked over and placed his hands on her shoulders. She glanced over her shoulder and up at him. She was a lot shorter than all of them, and looked so feminine standing there in the silk pink robe.

"Does this have something to do with your past, and why you didn't want to get involved with us?" he asked, and she opened her mouth but then closed it.

"No lies," Phantom snapped at her and crossed his arms in front of his chest.

"Yes."

"Well, explain it," Phantom said to her.

"No," she said and pressed away from them and walked around the bed.

Phantom reached out and pulled her into his arms. "Yeah, that response isn't going to fly, honey."

"Well it has to fly, because I'm not telling you anything else. You said to let go tonight. No strings attached, no complicated talking just feeling and I did. Let's not ruin this," she said.

Phantom didn't do vulnerable, but boy did her response send a sucker punch to his gut. This wasn't just sex. He knew the fucking difference. Why was she resisting and lying about what they obviously all felt?

"Don't lie. It was more than sex."

"It may have to be just that."

"What?" Mike asked, standing up and then stepping into his jeans.

"Something isn't right here. You're holding back and I get the feeling that whatever happened in your past that has you pushing us away and minimizing what we shared is going to be used by you as a wedge to keep your distance."

She ran her fingers through her hair. "I enjoyed spending this time with you," she said.

"No. You are not getting rid of us and putting up the fucking walls." Phantom lifted her up and pressed her back onto the bed. She straddled his hips, the robe parted and she reached up and cupped his cheeks.

"I don't want to, Phantom, but I will. To protect you," she said to him, and he squinted.

"To protect us?" Mike asked.

"Do you know what we do for a living, North?" Turner asked her.

"Turner," Mike warned him.

"No, I think she should know what we do. Maybe it will let her know that we're more than capable of handling whatever her fears are and whatever happened in her past," he added, and sat down on the bed and stroked her shoulder.

"We were in the military and are now hired by both government and military organizations to complete specified missions," Turner said.

"We're mercenaries," Phantom said to her, and her eyes widened.

"That's a secret we're willing to share with you to show you that we want this to work. That we can trust you and you can trust us," Mike said to her.

Phantom saw the tears fill her eyes. "Tell us. Give us some indication of how bad it was." He caressed her thighs and she held onto his forearms.

"I dated someone. A friend set us up. He was charming, wealthy and things seemed normal for several months, but soon I became his obsession," she said, and her nose turned red, a tear escaped her eye. His chest tightened.

"Was he abusive?" Turner asked.

"Yes." Phantom clenched his teeth.

"Were the police involved? Did you press charges?" Mike asked.

She shook her head. "It's complicated."

"How so? If he struck you and you got away, you press charges and he goes to jail," Turner said to her.

"You know that isn't how it works, and if that guy has connections, if you're held against your will and he doesn't let you leave, you can't report him," she said to him.

"He held you prisoner?" Phantom asked her.

Tears rolled down her cheeks. "I won't say more. I can't. I'm sorry, but that was way more than anyone knows. Your cousin Afina doesn't know. None of my friends do. I moved out here to be free, and to start a new life and hope that I never have to worry about him again."

"But you do worry? You think he'll come looking for you? That's why you have the gun?" Turner asked. She nodded her head.

"Where is he? What's his name?"

"No, Mike. I'm not telling you anything else. My fears are mine. I've come a long way from two years ago. Every day is a struggle to feel more confident and to not be afraid. I need that gun. Especially at night. I live in this apartment on the middle floor of the building for more reasons than the view and that I'm alone. No one can penetrate this apartment except through the front door."

"That's what all the deadbolts are about?" Phantom asked. He noticed them when he locked the door after they came inside. She nodded.

"No one can climb a ladder, and well, if someone was to come down on a rope and crash through the sliders, one, I have a gun, and two, they have to pass several windows before they made it to this one."

"Jesus," Turner said.

"Smart thinking. You don't need to be alone anymore. Not with us around. We can make that fear disappear," Phantom said and eased lower. He cupped her face between his hands and looked into her beautiful green eyes, at the tears on her lashes and he wanted to take all the fear and pain away from her.

"I accepted tonight because it felt so good to be in your arms. To have the three of you close, and that you said to let go and not think past the moment. I can't give more than what I gave tonight. I'm going to need slow, and you can't push me, because I know myself. When I get pushed into a corner and panic, I react, and I could get mean."

"Mean, huh?" Phantom asked, and cupped her breast.

"Yes."

"I can get intense, and I think with a little discipline you'll realize we care and we aren't going anywhere no matter how fresh you get," he said and pinched her nipple.

Her lips parted. "Phantom, please understand."

"I understand." He looked at Mike and Turner.

"We need you again, and again, and again, and eventually you'll realize how perfect this is and how perfect we are." He pressed his mouth to hers and eased the robe from her body. When he rolled to his back, she immediately took his cock into her wet pussy and began to ride him. She held his gaze. "Let go with us, and all the other stuff will fall into place."

She didn't respond verbally, but began to rock her hips as Turner moved in behind her and prepared her ass for his cock. Mike knelt on the bed with his cock in hand. "Together, so we secure this bond," he said, and she gasped as Turner eased a finger into her ass being sure she was ready to take him. In and out he eased that finger. She moaned and rocked back and forth up and down, and then he replaced fingers with his cock. He slid his cock into her ass and then lowered her mouth to Mike's cock. They rocked their hips, thrust into her over and over again, and Phantom watched her closely, feeling so much inside, and knowing that no matter how bad things were, he would do whatever it took to protect their woman, and help her to never feel pain or fear again. Everything.

* * * *

They were all moaning and thrusting into North and Turner was filled with too many emotions to analyze. Their woman, and North was their woman, had been a victim of abuse. That explained her knowing Ice, but he couldn't help but feel there was more to her story. As he thrust his cock into her ass, making love to her with Phantom and Mike, he knew this was different. That he never felt so compelled to take care of and possess a woman ever before. He understood what his friends in this type of relationship felt, he just worried about North's position in this, and whether she was so scarred that she couldn't fully give into them. There was so much to fear, yet so much more to enjoy. He gripped her hips and watched her suck on Mike's cock and counterthrust over Phantom.

"Ours. You're ours, North, always," he said and came in her ass. He hoped she felt his mark, his possessive hold on her body and her soul, because she sure got a hold of his heart, big time.

Chapter Six

"Are you going to inform Synista of this update?" Castella asked Ferlong.

Ferlong tapped his finger to his chin and leaned back in his chair at the desk.

Castella remained quiet.

"There are a few ways to play this. The money Sully asked for is well worth it. I mean, she's a beauty. Forester is obsessed with her. Her brother Tyler caused a lot of problems across the board for all of us. Then there's the aspect of involving ourselves in an abduction, and having cops on our asses."

"That's only if you do the abducting. I say if you're considering grabbing her, no matter what you decide to do with her, you make that scumbag agent do the dirty work for you. That way if or when Synista finds out, which you know he will because we're working that deal right now with the casinos, you can make it look like you were intervening to help save her and bring her to Forester."

"I like your line of thinking. I mean the woman means nothing to me, but her pictures, man she piques my curiosity."

"She's a fine looking woman, and controllable, too."

"I can get any woman I want, and Forester has been a good business associate, so there's no need to go after something he wants so badly. However, if we inform him of her location he could react and do something stupid. He's off the radar right now."

"Then he needs you to handle this, which means you could use it to negotiate the split on the deals with the casinos. You get a larger portion."

Castella raised one of his eyebrows up at him.

"Listen, any man would do the same thing. You don't need Forester to succeed in your business dealings, and he doesn't need you. The two of you have chosen to work with one another. I'm game no matter what you decide, and why? Because I know what I get out of this. The thing we need to worry about are the feds."

"That's what Dully is for. To falsify information and throw off the feds' scents. I think it's best we use this, her, as an added bonus to signing contracts and a deal with Forester."

"What about Loconto?"

"Let's hope Loconto doesn't find out about any of this, and about the woman. We know how he is. He would use her to control Forester and try to control us."

"Plus, if he got a hold of a woman like North, forget about it. She wouldn't survive."

Ferlong nodded. "She resists Sully and fights him taking her, I wouldn't put it past him to do his own kind of damage and deliver her."

Furlong exhaled. "Forester is obsessed with this woman. She's his weakness. We know it, Sully knows it, and if Loconto finds out, he'll want in on this, too, so let's keep it small. Contact Sully and give him the details, then let's sit back and let all the cards fall into place. The contracts and deals with the casinos, the drug deals, and the extra bonus money Forester will pay to get his precious woman."

"He'll pay whatever you ask. You know that, right?" Castella asked Ferlong.

"Sometimes the greatest warriors fall because of the loins of a woman."

* * * *

The morning after. Holy God she was nervous as she got dressed, which was a whole major decision because she wanted to impress them. Despite how many times they told her she was gorgeous, sexy, and how they loved her body, she was still uncertain, and felt self-conscious.

She knew it had a lot to do with what Forester had done to her. His words, his treatment of her, his capability of placing her on display and breaking her down. When she got dressed for work, for going out, or even just lounging in the apartment, she made certain she looked good. Forester demanded she always be ready to impress and look hot. She looked at herself in the mirror, the one piece sundress hugged her curves and dipped a little low in the front. There were a few buttons there and as she adjusted the dress she debated about unbuttoning another button, revealing more of her deep cleavage. That would be what Forester would want. He was one man she had to please, now she was involved with three. Three men who seemed mysterious, hard, commanding and superior in all aspects. Whether it be their physical appearances, or their commanding, ordering tones, they demanded respect and submission. She felt sick to her stomach. It was one night of making love. Hell, she had anal sex, multiple times. She loved every minute of it, but wondered what would come of this. Could they be serious or were they waiting in the kitchen for her to come out so they could break the news that last night and this morning were great, they had fun, and see ya?

Tears filled her eyes. She was an idiot. Fragile. More fragile than she was willing to admit or to reveal to anyone, even Ice. God, she would have to see Ice. She didn't tell Phantom, Mike, and Turner everything. She hadn't even touched the cruelty and abuse she sustained, never mind the danger she was still in. Could she never reveal that to them? Perhaps her luck would change and Forester would never find her?

She took a deep breath and exhaled. She could do this. She could do the morning after. She was strong, conditioned herself to hide emotions and her needs to be held and cherished. She was alone. That was the bottom line.

She walked out of her bedroom, her low-heeled sandals clicking on the tile flooring, and all three men looked at her. She stopped short. It was like she lost her breath at the sight of them alone. Phantom sitting on the bar stool by the island in the kitchen. His thick, muscular, jean covered legs out in front of him and one muscular arm leaning on the counter. That expression, so dark, unreadable gazed over her body and she felt it. Mike, gruff thicker than last night, button-down shirt unbuttoned but not too low, sleeves rolled up, one hand in his pocket and the other leaning on the counter behind him. His eyes swept over her. Turner. Oh heavens did he look hungry all over again, and he licked his lower lip and closed the space between them and snagged her around the waist. "You look incredible," he whispered, and suckled against her neck, making her shiver and her pussy cream once again.

She held onto his rock solid arms, feeling the protruding triceps and then smoothed her hand lower to hug him as he embraced her, and ran his palms over her ass and under her hair to her neck. He sniffed and she giggled. "You smell so good. I love whatever it is you wear all the time. I can smell it even if you aren't there," he said, and it shocked her. Those weren't words spoken by a man ready to say, "Adios, sweetheart."

"Want to go grab something to eat?" Mike asked, stepping closer as Turner pulled back but kept a hand on her hip.

She stared at them. "Are you sure you want to? You're not busy?"

Mike squinted at her and then reached out and cupped her cheek. "We don't want to leave you. We don't want our time together to end." Mike pressed his lips to hers. She kissed him back and decided it felt too good to be with these men to resist the attraction. She moaned into his mouth when she felt his hand slide up under her dress and then trailed a finger along the crack of her ass. He squeezed her ass cheek and she pulled from his mouth.

She pressed her cheek against his chest. "Or we could just stay here and make love all afternoon, and order in food," Turner said.

She pulled back and Mike slowly let his hand fall from under her dress. "I think we need to get to know one another more," she said, and slid her hands along her dress, only for Phantom to grip her wrist and pull her back against his front.

"Oh we're getting to know you. Every inch of you, sweetie. Including little beauty marks along your skin, and the tiny set of freckles along the back of your neck I can see when my dick is deep in your ass, and you're riding Mike, while Turner's cock is in your mouth," he said, lifting her hair and suckling on the spot she didn't even know existed, nor realized how sensitive it was until Phantom discovered it.

"Goddamn, we better leave now, or it's back to bed," Turner stated firmly.

Phantom lowered her hair and hugged her from behind, rocked his hips against her ass and she felt his erection. "Torture. It's going to be torture not touching you like I love to do because we'll be in public."

She exhaled and leaned back against him. "I feel it, too, Phantom, but things are moving so fast."

"Don't panic. We'll go to lunch, but you, little lady, are dessert." He gave her ass a smack and then led her toward the door. As she passed the island and the small table by the door, she grabbed her purse.

* * * *

"What are you guys carrying on about?" Sebastian asked the agents in the office. Monroe chuckled. "They've been talking about a text from friends of ours. They're semi-retiring and looking at some places down south."

"What are they sending you pictures of the homes?" Henry asked, moving closer to Monroe.

"No, the real estate agent is hot. The guys are talking about checking out the place," Monroe added, and pulled out his cell phone. "I swear I think Cortez is going to print out a picture of her and post it by his desk."

The guys chuckled.

Sebastian got a funny feeling in his gut as he walked over toward Henry and Monroe. When he saw Henry's eyes widen that feeling got worse. "Shit," Henry whispered, and sure enough as Sebastian checked out the picture his eyes locked onto North.

"Who saw this? How many guys?" he barked, and Monroe licked his lower lip. "By now I don't know. It's just me and five of the guys plus Rodriguez and Denver."

"I want all their names. Now," he said, and then walked away and looked at Henry, who he hoped would know what to do. Sebastian looked around the office and wondered if the rat was someone here or part of that group chat. It was a fear he had instantly. This is all it would take. One stupid fucking screw up and that was it.

He walked into the office and closed the door, but not before looking around the room. His eyes glanced toward the other set of open desks and then to Sully Frame. Immediately Sully looked away from him and toward the guys.

Sebastian listened to the phone ringing. He wondered why North wasn't picking up, and of course his mind ran to conclusions. What if someone got a hold of that picture and they already knew where she was and they informed Forester? "Pick up, North. Pick up the damn phone." He got her voice mail. He didn't want to scare her so he disconnected the call. He started to pace the room when Henry came in.

"I got a list of names, but there's no telling if there are others. These fucking guys forwarded it out."

"Shit. Why? What the fuck?" Sebastian asked and ran his fingers through his hair.

"She's a gorgeous woman, and she stands out. Guys will be guys."

He tried calling her again. "Well those guys unknowingly may have just ruined her life."

* * * *

North was smiling as she walked out of the ladies room. The guys were still at the table outside by the water and talking to a few friends.

They had met them and joined all of them for a drink afterward. Phantom wasn't too thrilled at all as he kept stroking her thigh and looking at her with hunger in his eyes. She was feeling sort of desperate to be alone with them again, but the crowd of friends grew bigger, and now Afina and Amelia were there, too.

She pulled out her cell phone as she made it to the doorway and the side door by the docks. She could see the table of friends and her men. Mike's eyes glued to her as well as Turner's and Phantom. She felt it everywhere. She saw the caller i.d. and smiled.

"Hi, Sebastian."

"'North, are you okay? All is good?" he asked, and she could hear the worry in his voice. She frowned and turned away from her friends.

"What's wrong?" she asked, her heart instantly sinking.

"Where are you?"

"Out with friends."

"Okay, listen, I don't know if this is a situation or not, but those guys, Rodriguez and Denver, they're agents that are part of another team who are friends with agents in this office. They took a picture with you and sent it to their friends, but now those friends are sharing the picture. It's out there, North."

"Oh God, seriously? Now what?"

"Honey, my thought about there being a rat in the agency could be accurate. Things have been going on. Henry and I went to do some undercover work and we have men we trust keeping eyes on things. We're getting closer to finding this rat because some things we planted, some orders for surveillance were intervened, and it was obvious someone informed the subjects that we would be watching. We're close, but now this situation, I don't know if it's a risk or what."

"Do I need to leave?" Her voice cracked and she felt scared, emotional. She didn't want to leave Phantom, Turner, and Mike.

"I don't know. I would be prepared to take action and initiate one of your plans of escape. Be ready. Be alert. Keep doing things with your friends and don't act suspicious where they'll worry about you and stay close. I know you fear them getting hurt."

"Oh God," she said, and thought of the men.

"What is it?"

"I met someone. Well, three men, and well."

"Fuck. It's serious?"

"I care so much about them."

"Did you tell them—"

"No, no of course not. I minimized it and made it seem like an abusive relationship."

"Who are they? I need their names. I need to look into them."

"Seriously?"

"I'm not taking chances on your life."

"You know them. You've already checked them out."

"What? Who?"

"Afina's cousins. Mike, Phantom, and Turner."

He whistled. "Wow, well to be honest, they're more badass than any agents that's for sure. Perhaps you may want to confide in them."

"No. No, Sebastian, I won't involve them in this. I can't do that. They don't deserve the trouble or to be killed protecting me. I'll put the plan into motion on your call, or if I feel like it is necessary."

"I'm so sorry."

"Do you think Rodriguez and Denver could be rats?"

"No, but Henry is checking things out. I would still take precautions."

"I feared this day would come. I knew I shouldn't have let my guard down and let them into my heart. I knew I should have resisted."

"We're close to catching these guys, North. When it's over, perhaps you'll be able to work things out with them. I want to come there, but if we're being watched it will lead them closer to you faster."

"No, I get it. I knew what this would be like when the time came. I got comfortable and I shouldn't have." She glanced back toward the guys and Turner was making his way toward her, obviously seeing her upset. "I need to go. Turner is watching and coming over."

"Be safe and be on guard."

"Will do," she said.

She looked out at the water and took several deep breaths when she felt Turner's arm come around her waist and hug her from behind. She grabbed onto his arm and leaned back.

She felt the tears in her eyes. She went and fell in love with them. Just like that.

"Are you okay? Who was on the phone?"

"No one important. Just some bad news."

"Bad news? What?" he asked, and kissed her neck.

"A contract fell through. One I thought was a sure thing. I guess I put too much confidence in it being a success."

"Don't worry, honey, they'll be others. You really take your job so seriously," he said to her, and she turned in his arms and pressed her hands against his chest.

She stared up at Turner, that gruff along his cheeks, those dark brown eyes. "Last night and today was amazing. I've never felt so happy, so safe," she said, and her voice cracked.

He squinted obviously picking up on her emotions. "Well, they'll be plenty more of them. We're never letting you go." He kissed her.

She hugged him tight, kissed him back, and focused on today and the rest of the night making love and being in their arms, for tomorrow she may have to disappear and she may never see them again, but at least they would live.

Chapter Seven

"I think he's double-crossing your boss, Synista. Ferlong was my contact and him and Castella want me to go grab North. She's alive and I know where she is," Sully said to Synista.

"Where?"

"Oh, I'm not saying yet. I'm the only one who knows right now and I want to cash in on this information."

"You know that Forester would pay you well for this."

"I'm getting fifty grand from Ferlong."

"What?" Synista yelled.

"Yup and I'm getting the cash when I have her in hand. What will you pay and I'll decide who I drop her off to."

"I need to talk to Forester. I'll call you back."

Sully smiled wide and ended the call. He sat there in his car, smirking. He was going to be a very rich man. He had to play his cards right though. It wasn't going to be easy to grab North, but perhaps he wouldn't have to deliver her like Furlong and Castella wanted him to. Perhaps Forester would send one of his own men to ensure she made it to wherever he was hiding out and living now. He didn't care. "Just show me the money."

* * * *

Mike lifted her dress up and over her head, tossing it onto the chair. Turner unclipped her bra and Mike held her arms above her head after her bra fell to the floor. She was naked, and looking so damn enticing he didn't think he would make more than a few strokes before he came.

He lowered his mouth to hers and kissed her as his brothers undressed.

Turner sat on the bed and lifted her up onto his lap so her back faced him and he spread her thighs. Mike lowered down. "Keep those arms up," he ordered, and she did until Turner pulled them back so she reached behind her and placed them around his neck best she could. The move caused her breasts to push out. Mike leaned up to nip one and tug on it as Turner stroked her cunt. Mike watched his brother's fingers dip into her wet pussy.

"Oh God, please. Please stop teasing me," she said, and Phantom moved closer. He was naked now, too, and cupping her breast. He leaned down to take a taste as Mike lowered and slid his palms along her thighs that were over Turner's thighs, and licked her from cunt to asshole. She wiggled and shook. Phantom gripped her chin.

"You ready to get filled up by your men?"

"Yes," she hissed, and he pressed his mouth to hers and then licked along her chin and neck to her breast. He sucked hard on it as Mike slid fingers to her pussy and her asshole.

"I get to fuck this ass, to slide my thick, hard cock into my woman and hear her beg for more," he said and stroked her. He pulled fingers from her and Turner slid his fingers into her cunt while sucking on her neck.

"You want that, North?" he asked.

"Yes. Yes." She thrust her hips forward.

"Let's do it," Mike said, and he stood up, took off his clothes as Phantom lifted her up, kissed her, then turned her around to ride Turner. She slid right over his cock, taking it into her wet, hot pussy and began to ride him. Phantom got up on the bed and gripped her hair.

"I need that hot, sexy mouth. I love this mouth," Phantom said, and kissed her then brought his cock to her lips. She lowered as she rocked her hips over Turner, and she took Phantom's cock into her mouth. Mike gripped her hips, saw how wet she was and he slowly fingered her asshole. "You ready?" he asked, and gave her ass a spank. She moaned and pushed back.

"Oh boy is she ready," Turner said, and Mike smirked, aligned his cock with her asshole and slowly began to push into her. He felt how snug and tight she was, as well as how deep, how powerful his emotions were. He loved how it felt being inside of her, making love to her with Turner and Phantom. They dreamt of one day having this. Of having a woman to love, to share, to grow old with and to protect and watch over. Knowing she was abused, and not knowing all the details made him feel a bit nervous. She would have to tell them everything, and it would have to be soon so he could give her what she needed to feel safe and loved like never before. "Oh fuck." He moaned as he slid his cock all the way in and began to thrust and rock into her ass.

They were all moaning, thrusting, rocking and it felt incredible. It felt like they were one and the emotions ran deep. He loved her. He fucking loved her. He thrust over and over again and Turner came, then Phantom, and North cried out her release and moaned and shook as she came, making Mike follow. He hugged her back, feeling spent but content. He pulled out and Turner rolled her to her back and began to kiss her breasts, her nipples and along her belly as Phantom grabbed a wet towel to clean her up. When they were done, they gathered around her on the bed, and he sighed. "How the fuck are we going to leave you tonight?" he asked, and stroked her thigh.

"How are we going to leave her ever?" Turner said.

"Maybe we won't. Maybe we'll stay just like this making love to our woman, only leaving every so often to eat," he teased, and then nipped her nipple. Mike saw her serious expression and she stroked his hair then looked at Phantom then Turner.

"We have to work, but know I feel the same way. I've never felt so loved, so cared for and protected ever. I never thought I could have happiness like this. You're all so amazing. I'll never forget this moment, this weekend, ever and how it got started," she added, but it sounded like a second thought, and Mike felt like she was going somewhere, but then she smiled and snuggled into Turner. He was instantly protective and possessive of her, and this was a first. He held his thoughts in his head and enjoyed the rest of the night with North, knowing that there were more days like this to come, and it wasn't over.

* * * *

"A hundred grand, and Gordo and Pulta will be there to grab her. You'll meet them outside the town and have a plan in motion."

Sully smiled wide. "Got it and it's a deal. I'll text her location, the town, her address, everything, and then where your men can grab her. You have my account number. When I see the transfer went through, I'll be there waiting," he said, and then ended the call. Sully typed away on the computer and after only one call, he found out the best place to grab her, an open house in two days. The location isolated and the only house on the block.

Now to make the drive and get there without anyone knowing wasn't going to be easy. He noticed that when Henry and Sebastian saw the group text with North's picture on it they went into complete panic. He had to keep ears and eyes on them as well, but how could he when he needed to leave tonight? He thought about it. A hundred grand. He could spare a little for some help. He would call one of the guys who was good at this shit. He could keep track of Sebastian and Henry, listen to their calls, and be steps ahead of them. Yeah, he could pull this off, and make it look like he headed to South Carolina to look at real estate like the rest of the agents all seemed to be doing, and with no knowledge that the real estate agent was hiding out there. He smirked and prepared to take action.

* * * *

"I'll see you when I'm all done. I know I have a lot of people interested in the property."

"I can get out of this training thing early and meet you there, maybe we can do a repeat of the last open house we caught you at," Mike said to her, teasing North over the phone.

She couldn't help but to smile, and at the same time, have a pit in her stomach. She looked at her bags packed and ready like she was leaving for a three-week vacation. She reorganized them and wanted quick access in case she needed to come back here to grab her things. "I don't think so. This place has surveillance cameras inside and outside. The owners are very wealthy."

"Okay then, we'll be getting out maybe a half hour after you're done and wrap things up."

"Well text me and we'll see where we can meet," she said, and then just kept hoping for another day, some more time with her men. Her men? They were hers and she was theirs, and she knew she needed to be honest with them and explain the situation, but if she did, they would get involved and then what? They would be in danger, too. She just couldn't do that. Plus, Sebastian was getting closer to catching the rat and catching Castella, Ferlong, and Forester. She could do this.

"Okay, let me get going. Talk to you later."

"Later," he said, and she ended the call, wishing she could tell him she loved him, but it was like she feared the time was coming where she would need to disappear. It wouldn't be fair and it would hurt too much.

She grabbed her things and headed out of her apartment and straight to the open house. The next several hours passed by pretty slowly.

* * * *

Forester looked at the pictures on the computer screen. His North looked stunning, even more beautiful than he remembered. Her blonde hair was longer, her skin color glowing and tan, and her body in even better condition than he remembered. She was coming to Costa Rica. He would have her back in his bed once again and under his control.

He reached out to trace the picture, but then clicked the mouse to look at the others. The picture of her between two men, the picture that finally proved she was alive and well and hiding in some small town in South Carolina.

Synista cleared his throat. Forester looked up at him.

"Did they arrive?" he asked.

"They are in South Carolina, their eyes on the house and on North. There are people viewing the house, as soon as they leave they'll move in."

"Excellent. I want to know when she is on the plane."

"What about Castella and Ferlong?"

"I made the call. They don't want beef between us or any trouble. They'll take care of Sully."

"What about the money you transferred?"

"It will be removed as soon as they take him out. Is the bedroom all set? I want to make sure she is comfortable. She'll be here for the rest of her life."

"It's all set, and the drugs are by the table. Merdock said he can go over the dosage to give her. She should still be out of it when she comes here."

"Gordo better not give her too much. I want her conscious when she arrives and sees that I found her and that her destiny was set from the start. Then when she resists, we can drug her up to train her."

"Everything will be perfect, Forester."

"I hope so. None have compared to her, Synista. None."

"Because she was meant to be your woman and now you will have her back, and you can focus on what needs to be done from here on out."

"Yes, I can sit back, enjoy this estate, my wealth, my power from afar, with a goddess by my side. Keep me posted on everything."

* * * *

North was wrapping things up, locking up the doors, making sure the windows were closed when she heard the front door open and close. "Hello, the open house is over," she said, and when he came around the corner she gasped. Gordo, one of Forester's men was there. She ran to the right, reaching for her purse.

"Don't run, North. You're coming with us. Hiding is over," he yelled to her, and she pulled out her cell phone and hit Sebastian's number and then grabbed her gun. She undid the safety and turned to see Gordo there pointing a gun at her. He lifted and shot. She shot, too, hitting him in the forehead, but never expected the pain in her arm and to get tackled to the ground by someone. Her gun went flying across the floor. "Fuck, North! Why?" he yelled and struck her. She screamed and she didn't know if Sebastian was on the line or not, but she started yelling out information.

"I killed Gordo, and I will kill you, too, Pulta!" she screamed.

"Stupid bitch. Move now."

"I'm shot."

"You're gonna be in worse condition than that when Forester gets his hands on you."

"No, no let me go. Where are you taking me?"

"You're going on a nice long flight to Costa Rica."

"No. No what is that? Don't." She screamed as Pulta shoved her onto her belly and stuck her in the neck with a needle. "By the time you wake up, you'll be in Forester's bed where you belong."

"No, leave me here. Leave me alone. Oh God. I can't see. Oh God." She cried as he dragged her from the house, her eyes landing on her cell phone on the floor, the gun feet away, blood from her arm trailing along with her and Gordo, bleeding from his forehead and dead. Sebastian will know who took her and where. She couldn't do anything else as weakness overtook her body and then darkness.

* * * *

"We can't let you in there," Rodriguez said as him and Denver blocked the taped off area leading to the house. There were police everywhere as well as paramedics, and the FBI.

"The fuck you can't. That's our girlfriend who is in there. We need to know about North. What the fuck is going on?" Mike demanded to know. Turner and Phantom were there too and trying to get through.

"She isn't in there, Mike. I can't get into the details and don't know too much, but I can tell you she isn't in there and it's a crime scene."

"A crime scene? What the fuck?" Turner yelled, and then Mike saw the men who looked like agents, two of them coming from the house. Denver looked at them. Mike locked gazes with the one guy. He was big, was clenching his teeth as he came closer.

"Let them by, Rodriguez," he said, and Rodriguez stepped aside and apologized for having to make Mike and them wait.

"Come over here with me please," the other guy said, and they followed and weren't sure of the situation, but it was obvious these guys knew who Mike and his brothers were.

"I'm Agent Mount, this is Agent Young."

"Where is North? What is going on?" Turner asked.

"There was a situation here today. Two men who have been searching for her got a tip from an agent, a rat inside the agency, and they came here to take her."

"What?" Phantom asked.

"Take her where and to who? What is this about?"

"I know she didn't tell you everything. She was trying to protect you. That's why she had a gun and she was able to kill one of the men."

"What?" Mike asked.

"Let me explain as quickly as I can. I know you'll have questions, but you're going to have to leave this up to us. Once we figure out where they took her in Costa Rica, then we can organize a rescue mission. There's a lot of red fucking tape here, and now with this crime scene, with the agent on the run that we know is a rat, we're about ready to arrest multiple big-time drug dealers."

"Holy fuck. I'm so confused. What the hell could North have to do with this?" Mike asked.

"Was her ex a drug dealer? The guy that was abusive?" Turner asked.

Agent Mount exhaled. "Let's go over here. We'll need time to sort things out, so I'll explain what's going on."

Mike was beside himself in anger and shock. As they stood there and listened to what North had been put through, how she nearly died, how her brother a traitor sold her out to this Forester dick, and how she was forced to be his woman and to suffer for over a year under his control. With every detail and as much informational Sebastian could give, they got a clearer picture of North's life and the secret she hid so well.

"No wonder she was so afraid to let down her guard with us," Turner said.

"She did though. When I spoke to her two days ago I knew she sounded different. I told her about the photo and it being shared, about the possible danger and she told me about you guys."

"You already checked us out. You know, at least have an idea from our credentials, what we're capable of," Phantom said to Sebastian.

"I do."

"So why wouldn't you tell her to confide in us? Why wouldn't she?" Turner asked.

"To protect you from Forester. Those men came here to kill whomever stood in the way of grabbing North. She knew that you would want to protect her, and the risk to your lives was something she wasn't willing to risk. This man hurt her so badly physically, emotionally, that I didn't think even with counseling she would recover. Never mind what her own brother did to her."

"It's understandable, but this was new between us and she had no clue as to what we do for a living. We also know who these men are. At least who Castella, Ferlong, and Loconto are. They're responsible for the murder of several of your agents and others. We were part of the team of mercenaries that destroyed that warehouse and factory in Peru," Mike told Sebastian.

His eyes widened. "Holy shit. Fuck, if Forester finds out."

"He won't find out because he doesn't know it was us. No one survived that but our team," Mike added.

"This is crazy. While you were doing that and killing these men, North was being beaten, drugged, and tortured. We got lucky when Forester sent her with two of his men to a discrete location and we stopped them before she could be forced elsewhere. We believe Forester was going to bring her out of the country," Sebastian told them.

Mike looked at his brothers and then at Sebastian. "We want in on this. Now whether you agree or not, we're calling in our people, our connections and we're doing this right. No offense, but you've had three years. We're experts at finding terrorist assholes hiding out in little fucking underground holes, we sure as shit can find this prick and his buddies in Costa Rica," Mike said, and then looked at Phantom. "Call the others. Have them meet us at the back room of Corporals," he said to him, and Phantom pulled out his cell phone and walked away.

"You can't get involved with this. We're hunting down three other main drug dealers that have killed numerous agents and have been bringing in illegal drugs and weapons to the United States," Henry said to them.

"Let me know who your commander is. We can work together or alone, but either way we'll be in Costa Rica by morning, and we'll have North back in our arms safe and sound, and this Forester guy under arrest or six feet under. All depends," Mike said.

"Depends on what?" Henry asked.

"If he's resistant, and if he hurts North."

"The government will not allow you to do this."

"The government won't know what the hell is going on and we'll be out of there before they even process the paperwork to start an investigation. Now are we doing this together or not?" Mike asked.

Henry exhaled and shrugged. "Together. All I ever wanted was to keep North safe and give her a chance at a normal life. The men need to go."

Chapter Eight

"You shot her?" Forester asked, looking at her arm covered in a bandage.

"Gordo shot at her when she pulled the gun and she killed him."

"Holy shit," Synista replied.

"That's a mess no one can clean up. The feds and the cops will be all over this shit," Pulta stated.

"We're taking precautions. No one will be able to find the estate, and if they did we would be aware of them long before they reach the perimeter. By that time, we can escape on helicopter if need be," Forester said and leaned down and stroked her cheek.

"She resisted some?"

"Yes."

"She'll suffer for killing Gordo. Let's get her comfortable. How long before the shit wears off?"

"An hour maybe. The doctor said it's a flesh wound and will heal. I didn't let him do stitches. Figured you may want someone better so she isn't scarred," Pulta said to him.

He nodded. "Leave us," he said, and they exited the bedroom. Forester looked at North. She was dressed nicely. Short, flare skirt, camisole and blouse that had blood on it. He reached for her, leaned down and inhaled against her neck. She still smelled the same. Delicious, sweet, and he removed the blouse and then looked at her abundant breasts. It was then as he trailed a finger along her neck that he saw the light marks on her skin. Love bites? He pushed the material down and sure enough there were more. Small marking, she was fucking someone. She had a lover? He shoved at her and stood up, running his fingers through his hair as he paced.

"Synista! Synista!" he yelled, and Synista appeared wide-eyed and concerned.

"She was fucking someone. Find out who. I want to know who?"

"Why? She's here now, what does it matter?"

"Look that this," he said, and pulled down her strap, revealing more of her breast, and pushing her head to the side, the love bites were faded but there.

He looked at Forester. "You really want to know? Then what?"

"Then I want him dead. I want him to know that I have her and she is mine and he can never fuck her again. Then slit his fucking throat."

"Okay," he said and bowed. Forester looked at North. He was fuming mad as he walked toward the closet and pulled out the ropes. He got to work. She was going to be punished the second she awoke. Punished for hiding from him, and punished for letting another man into her body. She belonged to him and him only.

* * * *

"Sully is dead. The body was found an hour ago," Henry told Sebastian, Mike, and the group of military men who gathered in the back room of their local bar.

"They catch them?" Watson asked, while Dell and Fogerty were looking at the laptops they had laid out on the tables. Ghost and Cosmo were on their phones and writing things down. Everyone was pitching in to help save North.

"Two got free. One is dead. How do you want to handle this, Sebastian?" Henry asked him.

Sebastian looked at Phantom, Mike, and Turner. "They could know exactly where Forester is holding North in Costa Rica. I need to question them."

"I'm coming along, too. There's no way we're wasting hours pampering these fucks. We do it mercenary style," Phantom said, and stood up. He adjusted his guns he had on his hip, his side, and motioned with his hand for Sebastian to lead the way.

"We should go, too," Turner said.

"No, you two stay here and organize our transportation and a team of men. We'll meet up to head out together. This won't take long," Phantom said to them, and Sebastian knew Phantom was the quiet one. How the hell was he going to question these guys? They headed out to the SUVs and were accompanied by a few other agents. When they got to the secure location, some empty house blocks from the bar, they headed inside. In a flash the tables were turned and shots were fired.

"Get down." Phantom grabbed Sebastian and pulled him lower, they nearly both got their heads blown off.

"Give up assholes, we got the place surrounded," Sebastian said.

"Not until the deed is done." The guy yelled out and shot at them again. Sebastian tapped Phantom's shoulder. "They got the place surrounded and more backup is coming," he whispered.

"We're not waiting," Phantom said, and he had his weapon drawn and he slowly started to make his way through the house.

* * * *

This whole operation was a shit show, and it seemed to Phantom and his friends that there were more agents involved with the illegal stuff and no one could be trusted. He certainly wasn't trusting anything these guys said or did.

"Phantom." He heard his name, turned and slid along the wall and peeked around the corner, and saw Henry being held at gunpoint by one of the prisoners.

"You're the boyfriend, right?" the guy asked.

Phantom kept his gun pointed at the guy, and he knew he could take the shot if need be, but then the guy spoke.

"You're the fucking boyfriend right?" he yelled and Sebastian joined him but remained hidden by the wall.

"Forester said to kill you, and let you know first that you'll never see North again, and never get to fuck her again, but he will, forever."

Phantom saw red. Henry moved slightly as the guy took his shot at Phantom and Phantom took his shot at the guy. Phantom watched as the guy's head splattered. Henry looked shocked and fell to the ground and Phantom could feel the burning on his ear. The fucker nearly took his head off.

"Holy fucking shit. Holy shit you shot him. You fucking shot him," Henry carried on, and Sebastian just looked at Phantom like he was crazy.

"Forester Colon and his crew of shit, are next," Phantom said, and walked out of the room and back to the SUV. That mother fucker sent men to kill him, but the guy said boyfriend, so maybe he didn't know about Mike and Turner, but Forester knew she was intimate with them. Considering what they heard about this guy's obsession with her and how he put her in the hospital, he surely would take out his anger on North. They had to get to her. They needed to leave as soon as possible.

* * * *

Turner and Mike grabbed onto Phantom the moment he got back to the bar. "Are you okay? Holy fuck, your ear is bleeding," Turner said, and Ghost came over with Fogerty.

"Let us take a look and then bring you up to date. You explain what the fuck happened first," Mike said, and he explained and everyone got more angry and even somber.

"He'll hurt her. He'll make her suffer," Ghost whispered.

Henry and Sebastian came into the room. "This is out of control, we got men prepared and in position to raid numerous buildings where we know Castella and Ferlong reside. We don't want to move in on them yet in case they warn Forester and then he moves North and goes somewhere we can't locate her. He has resources and in that country, he could be in the middle of the fucking jungle," Sebastian told them.

"Well, we aren't waiting. We've got a plane stocked, fueled and ready. We got people on the ground in Costa Rica we trust, and men working on locating exactly where Forester is." Mike said to him.

"How the hell could you have people there looking and a plane all set and ready? We don't even have an approval from the agency to plan and initiate a search and rescue."

"Your commander has been overruled. This has become a mission of special operations unit. The approval comes as we organize and facilitate the mission to confiscate illegal weapons, narcotics, and paraphernalia that was illegally transported overseas by one terrorist cell led by Forester Colon. His name is on a wanted list of terrorists in connection to various crimes and murders. Due to the fragility of this international invasion, no federal agents will be involved and it will be accomplished by a secretive set of individuals who take out terrorist for fun. Now enough of the bullshit. You in or are you out?" Mike asked.

"Fuck yeah I'm in. North deserves a life and to be free from all this shit her brother caused. She needs her men."

"Let's do it," Turner said.

And they started issuing orders and organizing the series of events and what teams would be going.

Mike placed his hand on Phantom's shoulder and his other hand on Turner's shoulder as they stood by the wall. "This is crazy shit, right here under our watch, in our territory our woman was taken. God only knows what she's going through right now and how alone and scared she is. We use that to fuel our mission, to achieve success, and to bring these assholes down. You know as well as I do who these fuckers are and what they did to members of our organization and to us more than two years ago. While we were fighting to save our fellow soldiers, North was being taken and about to be forced onto a plane when we were fighting for our lives against these same assholes. They're going down. Our commanders know and approve. It ends in Costa Rica."

"Fuck yeah," Phantom stated.

"Let's go get our woman, and when this is over, we're not letting her out of our sight," he said, and they nodded before they headed out to the waiting vehicles.

* * * *

"Noooo!" North screamed as Forester struck her with the belt. He made the mistake of untying her hands, and tried forcing her to hug him and lay in the bed with him. She could hardly move she was so bruised up, and her cheek throbbed, her eye was swollen, she was weak from the assault and from the drugs he gave her. She scratched at his face, ripping his skin. He roared and backhanded her in the mouth and she flew back, hitting the floor. Her head was numb, her mind a whirlwind of crazy thoughts as she rocked back and forth and growled at him.

"What the fuck?" Synista said, coming into the room.

"The fucking drugs. What the hell did you give her? How much Forester?" he asked.

"Just enough to calm her, to make her relax in my arms."

"She's having a reaction. Some people become violent on that shit."

"Fuck! I need her to accept me. I need to know that man is out of her head and he is dead. You got word, right? Phantom is dead?" Forester asked.

She understood everything he was saying. She didn't know what they gave her or what was in the drugs but she felt bursts of anger and didn't feel a thing as she attacked. Forester grabbed her arms and yanked her back onto the bed. "Help me tie her up. Then I'll give her some of the other stuff until I can figure out a plan," he said, and she tried fighting them and she was screaming at them to let her go. To get away from her. She had no more voice. It was hoarse and her throat burned from screaming and fighting.

"You didn't answer me. Is Phantom dead? Is her boyfriend dead?" Forester asked, and Synista stared at her as Forester prepared another needle. This time he got something from a purple velvet packet.

"He's no longer a problem," Synista said, and tears fell from her eyes.

They killed Phantom. She got Phantom killed. Mike and Turner would hate her. She had nothing to live for. Nothing. Her eyes rolled and the room spun. She slid her head side to side and felt Forester's hand against her cheek.

"Stop fighting your fate, North. I own you. I own this body, this soul, and every inch of you will be mine and you will obey my commands. Your boyfriend is dead, and any other man who tries to take you from me will die a horrible death as well," he said to her and she stared up into his dark eyes, watched him as his lips pressed to hers, and she felt numb once again.

She was losing her fight to live. *I killed Phantom.* She closed her eyes, felt Forester's palms along her belly then her thighs and to her breast. She focused on feeling numb, and putting up the walls so she would get through his games and hopefully meet death soon enough.

Chapter Nine

Eight days. He's had her for eight whole fucking days. What has he done to her? Where the fuck is he? How could no one get this right? I'm not giving up, North. I know this is going to be the spot. We're close. I feel it.

Phantom was right behind Mike and Turner. Watson, Dell, and Fogerty were in position and they were waiting for confirmation. A tip from a friend who lived out this way had picked up on several trucks delivering supplies. He found it odd, until his hunch paid off as he did some recon and saw the guards around the perimeter of jungle, video surveillance, and then a residence in the distance. He got through security to get a closer look and sure enough he saw a man who appeared to be one of the men they were looking for. Pulta. He took photos and sent them to Watson, and here they were, desperate for this to be the spot.

He was tired, angry, they all were, but they needed to be sharp and on their toes. They had fifteen men with them. Friends, some familiar with the territory, and of course Sebastian. Castella and Forester were arrested, but their lawyers were doing their thing and Sebastian didn't know if anything would stick. What they had on Forester would, and definitely the crime of abduction, assault and fuck he didn't want to think about the possibility of rape. It made him sick.

"We're getting ready. When we get the signal, we move quickly and carefully. Our objective is to kill anything in our path and to find North. Forester has connections to international terrorist and recently negotiated a deal with some Iranian assholes. The U.S, government has evidence. He's going away for life. Unless he wants to go out in a blaze of glory, then we'll provide that blaze," Mike said, and they all agreed.

"Mic check," he said, and they all made sure their ear pieces were working. "Teams of three. On my signal." He then pressed his finger to his ear. About ten seconds later, spotlights went out, small sparks illuminated throughout the estate property and they moved in.

"Pop, pop, pop, pop." Phantom fired his weapon, so did Mike and Turner. They were all moving along swiftly, taking out the enemy, and above in the trees they had their friends sniping out more men who came to fight against them and stop them. They made it into the house in record speed. Dell, Fogerty, Watson and the others along with Sebastian got through. Phantom, Turner, and Mike moved up the stairs, their friends moved along the living room, others came in across the deck and onto the roof. Phantom could hear yelling and then more gunfire. When they got to the hallway and there was one large wooden door, he knew that North had to be in there. The bullets hit the door and they ducked for cover. As the door burst open, there stood Forester and Pulta firing their semi automatic weapons. They fired back as both men emerged, but then Forester ran back into the room, Pulta went down as they shot him up with bullets and then Forester reappeared, holding a very beaten, bloody woman in his arms around her waist. It hit him insanely that it was North. She could hardly stand up, and Forester kept pulling her higher. He held the gun on them with one hand. "I'll kill her right now.

"North, don't move!" Phantom yelled to her, his gun pointed at Forester as well as Mike's gun, Turner's gun, and numerous other guns. She rolled her head to the side and then it was like she saw Phantom and her eyes widened. He didn't even see the knife she had, and suddenly she turned and stabbed Forester in the chest. He roared and turned the gun on her. The bullets sprayed erratically and they all took aim at Forester, but as he fell, North was hit with a bullet and she went down to the ground.

"Nooo!" Phantom roared and him, Mike and Tuner went running toward her. They looked at her battered body, her pale complexion, and the blood oozing from her chest.

"Apply pressure. We have to get her out of here. We can get help off this estate, have a helicopter pick her up. I'll get on that come one and move." Watson yelled and Phantom lifted her up, Mike applied pressure to her wound and blood was all over them.

"Come on, North. Fight damn you. Come on,'" he yelled and they carried her out of the house and through the jungle to the clearing.

"I can hear them. Your buddy. He's a pilot. He'll get her to the hospital," Watson informed them, and they got her to the chopper as it landed.

"Two, that's all I can fit with her," the pilot said.

"You go, Phantom. We'll get there.

"I'll go, too. I can get her the best medical attention around. I'll call it in," Sebastian said, and they agreed and Phantom held onto his brothers' somber gazes, and then looked down at North. She was so badly bruised and beaten. He felt the tears in his eyes and the anger boil up as Sebastian kept pressure on the wound and made calls on the satellite phone.

"You have to make it, North. You have to," Phantom said, and then looked at Sebastian.

"She'll make it. She's tough, and she loves you guys. She'll make it."

* * * *

"Well, anything yet?" Mike asked and him, Turner, and the team all arrived, filing into the small emergency waiting room. Phantom shook his head.

"Fuck," Mike said and paced.

"She's in surgery as we speak," Sebastian told them.

"What did they say? Do these people know what the fuck they're doing?" Turner asked.

"Yes, she has an excellent surgeon. When I called the situation in there just so happened to be a top surgeon staying at one of the local resorts. All we can do is pray now," Sebastian said to them.

The hours passed and nothing. Not a word, until suddenly, the doors to the emergency room staff only opened and there stood a doctor. He had sweat stains on his neck and was wiping his brow. He locked gazes with Phantom and then Sebastian. "She's alive," he said to them, and sighs of relief went through the room.

Phantom, Mike, Turner, and Sebastian stepped closer. "Will she make it?" Sebastian asked.

"It's going to be touch and go for a bit, but she definitely has the will to live. We almost lost her a few times on the table."

"Jesus," Turner said, and ran his fingers through his hair.

"I believe she'll make it. She has a fight in her that's for sure. A hair more, and no amount of fighting would have saved her. The main impact of the bullet was to her shoulder bone. They'll be other surgeries ahead of her, but the next twenty-four hours are crucial and will tell us a lot."

"Thank you, Doc. Thank you so much for everything you've done," Mike said, and shook his hand.

"I'm glad I was close by. I'll be here, and if need be, I'll extend the trip to ensure she can travel back to the states. Like I said, a lot depends on the next twenty four hours."

The doctor walked away with Sebastian and Phantom, Mike and Turner hugged and their buddies were right there with them.

"She'll pull through. She's a fighter," Watson said.

"She'll make it. Look at what she did. She fought even under drugs and exhausted and killed that asshole," Dell added.

"Sure the fuck did. She's badass like you three, and that's the kind of woman you deserve. She'll be just fine," Fogerty said, and then the others shook their hands and prepared to stay right there with them until they were certain North would live.

Epilogue

North awoke to the sounds of the ocean, and a gentle breeze that caressed her bare thighs. She took a breath and breathed in the scents of her men's cologne. She was at their house recovering, and getting pampered and cared for. She had been exhausted after making love to them and then showering. She laid down for a nap and still only wore one of Turner's button-down shirts and nothing else. She brought the collar to her cheeks and turned her head to inhale the scent of him when the floor creaked.

"Nice nap?" Mike asked, and then Turner and Phantom came in behind them. They only wore their jeans, no shirts, and those muscles, and sexy expressions had her body all ready to make love again. She moved and felt the slight ache, and their eyes furrowed and they were up on the bed, Mike cupping her cheek, Phantom sliding in behind her and pulling her against his chest.

She smiled. "I'm fine."

"You're pushing yourself too much," Turner reprimanded. "Nonsense. I'm fine, just get tired after making love to my men. I'll be good for tonight," she said to them as there were plans to meet everyone at Corporal's for a celebration they never had the chance to have. But really she wanted to see Amelia and talk to her. Something was going on with her, and when she visited at the hospital after North was transferred to one here in Mercy, Amelia had a hard time seeing her bruises. She asked her questions about fighting, about shooting a gun, and about how feeling confident and capable. She hoped that Cavanaugh wasn't still harassing her. Then of course she was also worried about April. She disappeared not too long after North was transferred to the hospital and she stayed away for a few weeks and didn't tell anyone where she went or whom she was with. She really needed to get back into the swing of things despite her recovery process.

"Maybe tonight isn't such a good idea," Phantom said, and kissed her neck and then rolled her to her back and slid over her. She straddled his waist. "Well, we could stay here and make love all night, but I think our friends are getting mad about not seeing us. It's been months."

"Who cares?" Phantom asked, and she chuckled and gave his arm a slap but felt the ache in her shoulder and winced.

"Fuck," Mike said, and then kissed her bare shoulder where the shirt was falling.

"We need to get ready."

Phantom kissed her and began to ease his fingers up into her cunt, making her moan.

"Oh God, we are going to be late."

"Mmm, yes we are," Mike said, and stepped from his jeans just as Turner did and they prepared to make love to her again.

Over an hour later they arrived at Corporal's and received welcome cheers and hugs from everyone. It was in that moment as she looked around at the people, some she knew well, most she only knew by their names but not their stories. There had to be a hundred different stories in this place tonight, and hers was only one. She looked at her men and smiled. Mercy changed her life. Her friends, her lovers, all helped to give her life and give her the will to fight to keep it. Her past was behind her and her future was right here in Mercy, right here in her lovers' arms, surrounded by friends, and those she called her family.

THE END

WWW.DIXIELYNNDWYER.COM

Siren Publishing, Inc.
www.SirenPublishing.com